Gray Love
A Black and White Affair

Copyright © 2011 Maya Seymour

ISBN 978-1-61434-298-4

All rights reserved. No part of this publication may be reproduced, stored in a retrieval system, or transmitted in any form or by any means, electronic, mechanical, recording or otherwise, without the prior written permission of the author.

Published in the United States by Booklocker.com, Inc., Bangor, Maine.

The characters and events in this book are fictitious. Any similarity to real persons, living or dead, is coincidental and not intended by the author.

Printed in the United States of America on acid-free paper.

Booklocker.com, Inc.
2011

First Edition

Contributing Editor: Kathryn M. Tedrick

Gray Love
A Black and White Affair

Maya Seymour

To my beautiful mother, Ruby

Chapter One

Taylor Henderson lounged in his brown leather recliner, watching the day's market news. His attention occasionally wandered to the banner scrolling across the bottom of the screen with the day's stock market results. His wife Jill was stretched out on a chintz upholstered sofa, reading James Patterson's latest novel. Henderson worked for a local brokerage, which was a branch of one of the largest firms in Mississippi. Earlier that week, he had been surprised when his boss shook his hand and told him he had been promoted to head investor.

The position came with a sizeable raise and meant that his wife could quit her job as a maid for the Richards' family. Jill had given her two-week notice the following morning. Although Mrs. Richards had not yet found a suitable replacement, she did not mind staying on until a new maid was found. Soon she would be able to spend more time cooking her husband's favorite meals, caring for her home, and playing with their two adorable children.

Swoosh! The sound startled them only seconds before orange light flared in the front lawn of their home. Wearing a white t-shirt, black drawstring shorts, and no shoes, Taylor jumped up from his chair and headed for the huge picture window, but when he reached it, he ducked and jerked back as something shattered the glass, showering him and the room with deadly projectiles. Taylor threw his arms up in front of his face, but that didn't save his arms or bare feet from being ripped by the razor-sharp shards of glass.

Heading for the hall closet at a half-run, and trailing bloody footprints across the hardwood floor, Taylor yanked open the closet door, and grabbed his shotgun and a box of shells. Then he crept back to the window, ignoring the pain in his arms and feet when he caught sight of the tableau on his front lawn. What he saw made his curly black hair stand on end.

Shadowy figures in white robes and hoods moved around a gigantic flaming cross like demons dancing around the fires of hell. Sparks flew through the air as the wood burned savagely and neighbors drew curtains across their windows, pretending not to see what was happening. Black or white, it didn't matter. No one wanted to become involved and risk turning the Klan's anger against themselves and their families.

Ignoring the blood trail across the floor caused by his bleeding feet, Taylor rushed around the room turning off lights and the TV, as Jill quickly shook the glass out of her shoes and slipped them on. She had been fortunate. None of the glass had reached her exposed skin, thanks to her husband, whose body had shielded her from most of the blast.

"Jill, grab the kids and get to the basement."

She hurried toward the children's room and found them huddled together in the hallway shivering with fear and uncertainty.

"What's happening, Momma?" her nine-year-old son T.J. asked.

"It's okay, baby, everything is going to be all right, but you have to do exactly what I tell you. Okay?"

The son nodded as she took his little sister's hand. Outwardly calm, Jill led the frightened children to the basement door, ordering them down the stairs.

"Go to the play room where there are no windows and lock the door. You can turn on the light and play, but don't come out until I come get you. Understand?"

"Yes, Momma," the children replied.

As soon as they were safely locked in the play room, Jill locked the basement door and returned to the living room.

"Jill, I told you to go to the basement," Taylor said, his voice edged with fear.

"Bullshit," his wife answered as she grabbed his hunting rifle off the shelf, knocking a box of shells over in the process. "The children are safe. My place is here with you." Jill expertly loaded the weapon and held it to her chest, muzzle pointed upward. "My daddy taught me to shoot when we went hunting. I'll show those bastards a thing or two about how to use a rifle."

Taylor didn't have time to look at her, but his heart filled with pride. He crawled to the destroyed window, doing his best to avoid the minefield of broken glass. Then carefully rising, he peeked over the windowsill.

"Taylor Henderson, come outside, boy, and receive a message from the Lord," a deep, somewhat familiar voice shouted, ringing loud and clear through the windows of the home. "The Bible says that Israel shall stand alone and be God's chosen race. You are evil, straight from the devil himself, and shall not be tolerated!"

Jill inched up behind him. "Fine talk coming from a bunch of Klansmen," she whispered. "They hate Jewish folk almost as much as they hate us."

Taylor crouched alongside the wall next to his wife, peeking out the window from time to time to check the Klan's movements. Jill leaned close to him, pressing her sweaty face against his white t-shirt, her bravado smothered by fear.

"Lord, please make those people go away from here," she prayed softly. "Don't let them hurt my babies or my man."

"Shush, baby," Taylor said, patting her cheek. "We're going to be fine. They're just trying to scare us."

"Well they're doing a mighty fine job of it," Jill replied sarcastically.

Her spurt of bravado brought a brief smile to her husband's lips, but his features turned grim when a bullet crashed through the bay window in the dining room. Glass flew inward, spreading jagged slivers across the room that glittered in the light of the fire. The bullet lodged in the front of the marble fireplace across the room with an audible thud. Jill shrieked, raising her hands as if to protect herself, and her rifle hit the floor with a heavy thump, harmlessly discharging into the opposite wall.

"Boy, you best come on out before we have ta come in there and git you," another voice shouted above the roar of the flames. "We know your woman works for Mrs. Richards down the street. If we don't git you tonight, we'll git her tomorrow. Come out and face us like a man."

Taylor flinched. His wife was curled into a ball on the floor. Stark terror edged the whites of her dark eyes, and his heart constricted. *No,* he thought. *I'm not hiding behind my wife's skirts. I can't risk her safety, especially knowing what they would do to her.* Gripping the shotgun tightly, he rose and headed for the front door.

"No, Taylor, please," Jill screamed. "Don't leave me! They'll kill you!"

He glanced back at her, taking in every feature of her beautiful face, knowing he may never be able to look upon it again. "Don't worry, sweetheart," he whispered. "No matter what, I'll always be with you." Without another word, he flung the door wide and stood in the opening, wearing nothing but shorts and a t-shirt. "You bastards don't scare me," he shouted. "Get away from here." Raising the weapon, he fired a warning shot across the yard.

Their response was a fusillade of bullets that tore through Taylor Henderson like daggers through paper, causing his body to jerk spasmodically. In shock, he looked down at his chest, surprised at the blooming red stains spreading across his white t-shirt. Somewhere to his left, Jill cried out, but it seemed like her voice was miles away. His legs crumpled, and Taylor dropped to the floor, saved only by her arms around him. He heard her sobbing as she held a cordless telephone to her ear and gave someone their address.

His last thoughts were of the warmth of his wife's arms, the softness of her breasts, and the faint sound of sirens wailing in the distance.

Chapter Two

"I don't understand why they did this, Chief," Lieutenant Geoffrey Tray of the Crystal Springs, Mississippi Police Force said as he slammed his fist against the top of the Chief's desk. Frustration made his normally gentle features harsh with anger. Tall and built like a linebacker, in the thirty-eight years he had lived, he had never been afraid because of his race.

Chief Ron Waldron's thick white hair and piercing blue eyes were a direct contrast to Geoff's dark good looks. Waldron was a down to earth type of guy with excellent family values. There was nothing he would rather do than play catch with his grandsons or bounce one of his young granddaughters on his lap. The older man leaned back in his desk chair, his wiry frame relaxed against the worn brown leather. Waldron had a reputation for being a fair, civil-minded man who didn't tolerate crime, especially crimes of hate, and at sixty-five, he had pretty much seen it all.

"You know why they fixated on Henderson, don't you Geoff?" he asked. "It's because he was moving up in their world, and they didn't want him there."

Waldron leaned forward and picked up a folder from the corner of his desk, filled with photos and the initial reports taken at the scene. After a quick glance, he slid the open folder across the desk toward Geoff. The Lieutenant glanced at the top photo but did not touch it.

"Chief, that man wasn't a threat. He wasn't active against the Klan and stayed mostly to himself. Taylor never stuck his nose in anybody's business but his own." Geoff dropped into the hard wooden chair in front of the Chief's desk. "All he wanted was to provide a decent living for his family, same as everybody else."

"The Klan doesn't care who you are or what you do, Geoff, unless you're black, and then you had better stay in your place." Waldron shook his head. "They didn't like the idea that Taylor Henderson would be making six figures." He stared at the Lieutenant. "Any ideas about the individuals behind this?"

"Not really." Geoff met the older man's gaze, searching for a reaction to his next words. "I've heard rumors that some pretty powerful and influential citizens of Crystal Springs belong to the Klan." He pushed the file back across the desk.

Waldron leaned back in his chair and decisively closed the folder. "Got any names?"

After a moment, Geoff sighed. "How would anyone know for certain? The Klan hides behind those hoods so that no one knows who they are. They do their dirty work, and then go about their lives, smiling and pretending they're perfectly upright citizens, who would never dream of harming a fly, let along murder a man in cold blood."

"You're right," Waldron agreed, his brow furrowed. "This is the second Klan murder of a black man this month. It has to stop now before any more decent folk end up dead. We need to go all out on this one. Are you up for it?"

"Are you assigning the case to me, Chief?" Geoff desperately wanted to be the one to bring the KKK to justice.

"It's all yours, but first let's do what needs to be done for Jill Henderson." Waldron held the folder out to Geoff.

Geoff took it. "I'll do my best for the Henderson family," he promised. "My wife called to tell me that the community has put together some donations to help out, and Mrs. Richards told Jill she could have her old job back."

"When's the burial?" The Chief pulled a notepad out of his drawer and reached for a pen.

"Friday at ten," Geoff told him.

"I'll be there," Waldron said. "I assume you'll be there as well?"

"Sure, Chief, Rosie and I are friends of the family." Geoff stood up to leave, anxious to get started on the case.

Waldron stopped him. "One more thing, Geoff, start by questioning Ken Lewis at the car repair shop down on Gibson Street. Rumor has it that he may be a member of this group. I sure would like to know who's supplying the money for their operation."

Geoff nodded. "I'll see what I can dig up, Chief."

"And Geoff?"

"Sir?"

"Be careful. That badge may not be enough to protect you. We don't know what this group is capable of doing. Men that hide their identities under a hood might find it a bit too easy to kill a police officer, especially a black one."

Geoff nodded and headed out to his unmarked police car. He wondered how he could handle the investigation without seriously ruffling someone's feathers, but was fresh out of ideas. If Lewis was involved in the killing, he would never admit it. When the Lieutenant arrived at Lewis's garage, it appeared deserted, but as he parked his car and approached the building, the garage owner met him at the door.

"Afternoon, Lieutenant," Lewis said, wiping his hands on a tattered, red, oil-stained rag. "What brings you here?" He glanced at Geoff's Chevrolet, a crooked grin on his face. "Somethin' wrong with your car?"

"I'm not here about my car, Ken," Geoff replied, keeping his voice neutral. He focused on the slender middle-aged man, wondering if white sheets suited him better than the jeans and dirty blue shirt with his name neatly stitched in red over the left pocket.

"What do you want then? I'm a busy man." Lewis brushed back a lock of greasy black hair, leaving a smudge across his forehead. He nonchalantly picked up a large wrench from a nearby toolbox and tapped his thigh with it a few times. At five-seven, he had to look up to see Geoff's face. The Lieutenant did not miss the implied threat. Lewis's dark eyes furtively darted about the garage, as though searching for a safe place to hide.

"I'm here about the Henderson murder," Geoff said, trying to gauge Lewis's reaction.

The other man looked away under the cop's steady stare. "Oh, you mean that black investor fellow, right?" Lewis replied, relaxing just a bit. "Too bad about him, family must be all broken up."

"You knew him?" Geoff asked, looking for some telltale sign that his questioning was headed in the right direction.

"News travels fast in a small town like this." Lewis offered a smile that was suspiciously similar to a smirk. Still carrying the wrench, he headed toward a late-model silver Toyota, sitting in front of the garage with its hood up.

"Heard anything about who's involved?" Geoff asked, following a few steps behind.

Lewis glanced back at the deputy shadowing him. "Even if I did, what makes you think I'd tell you? You think I want the Klan comin' after me?"

Geoff felt his professional composure slip. He kept his voice even, but it took a lot of effort. "I was hoping you would cooperate. That's all."

"Hope is such a sad word, ain't it?" Lewis laughed nervously. "Besides, that's all I know, so I *am* cooperatin'."

Geoff gave Lewis a hard look, using his best attempt at official scorn. Then he turned and walked back to his car, his fisted hands stuffed deep in the pockets of his uniform pants. He spent the rest of the afternoon following one dead-end lead after another. By five o'clock, he had a migraine of gigantic proportions and wanted nothing more than to go home to his sweet wife. In spite of the pain thudding against his skull, he decided to stop and pay a visit to Jill Henderson. He had known the Hendersons for years, and he hoped that Jill would be okay.

Turning down the street to the Henderson home, Geoff slid the car to a stop along the curb in front of the frame house. Taylor had kept the home in tiptop condition and had given it a fresh coat of white paint only last month. The boarded up picture window was a dim reminder of the tragedy that had occurred there the night before. Getting out of his car, the Lieutenant walked up to the front porch and rang the bell.

A few moments later, Jill opened the door, wearing a black dress usually reserved for Sundays. She looked surprised to see him. "Geoff?"

He noted the dark circles under her eyes and the redness that always came from crying a lot. "How are you holding up, Jill?" He reached out and pulled her into a comforting hug.

After several seconds, she stepped back so he could enter the small tiled foyer. "Come in, please."

"I just wanted to tell you how sorry I am for you and your family," Geoff said, taking a seat on the rose-patterned sofa she had occupied the previous night.

"Sorry for what?" She looked down at him, her face etched with sorrow. "You didn't take my husband away from me. I never dreamt the Klan would do something like this. We never bothered anybody. Why couldn't they have just left us alone?"

"I don't know, Jill. I wish I had answers for you," he replied, wondering where the children were. The house was too quiet. "How are the kids taking it?"

"Taylor Junior is devastated," she said. Turning to look out the window, she seemed to drift into her own thoughts. "Yeah, T.J. loved his daddy. Everywhere his daddy went, T.J. was right behind. Little Brianna is only three, so she'll be okay. My mother has them right now."

Geoff didn't know how to comfort her, or what he could say to make things better.

She turned back to him, tears shimmering in her eyes. "It's my son I'm worried about. The boy is scared out of his mind. He hates the fact that in two days, his daddy will be lying in the ground." She dabbed at her tears with a clean white handkerchief.

"T.J. will be okay. He's a tough kid. The boys at the precinct and I will look after him, get him into football. That's what he wants to do."

"Yes, that will help, I think." Jill gave him a questioning look. "I know you didn't come just to see how we were doing," she said, giving him a wan smile.

"You're right. I hate to put you through this again, but can you tell me what happened last night?" Geoff asked, reaching into a jacket pocket for his notebook and pen.

Jill remained silent for so long that he began to think she hadn't heard him. Finally she said, "Taylor and I were relaxing before going to bed. We were both tired and wanted to unwind a little. At around ten-thirty, we heard something... a kind of whoosh in the front yard." Her breath caught in a sob. "I'll never forget that sound. The flames looked like something out of hell, an insult to the meaning of that cross. Someone threw a rock through the living room window. There was glass everywhere, and Taylor went for his gun in the hall closet. He was barefoot, his poor feet cut and bleeding from all that glass."

Geoff saw the pain in her eyes as she forced herself to repeat the details so vividly imprinted in her brain, her hands wringing the handkerchief into a tight knot.

After a moment, he prompted her. "How many cars were there?"

"I saw at least two cars and a truck," she said softly. Geoff wrote as she talked.

"When I saw those vehicles out front, I woke the children, sent them down the basement to the playroom, and locked them in, so they would be safe."

He looked up when she paused again, but after a moment, she went on.

"Taylor grabbed his shotgun and told me to go to the basement, too, but I refused. I got his rifle and loaded up. When I looked out the window again, I saw at least a dozen robes, and I think there was another car closer to the porch."

"What can you tell me about the vehicles?"

Her eyes closed a moment, as she visualized the nightmare scene of the previous evening. "A red Mustang, an old Chevy truck, and a station wagon," she replied, opening her eyes.

"Color and make of the station wagon?"

"I think it was black or maybe dark blue, but I don't know what make it was, but it was old."

"Okay. Go on," Geoff gently prodded.

"They yelled for Taylor to come out, and when he didn't, they started screaming about coming after me, saying they knew where I worked. That upset Taylor and made him angry."

Fresh tears flowed down her cheeks. "I begged him not to open the door, but he wouldn't listen, stubborn fool. He fired a shot over their heads to scare them, but they fired back. The sight of his body jerking when those bullets tore into him will haunt me for the rest of my life."

Geoff nodded, imagining the explosive scene. He knew it wouldn't do any good, but he asked anyway. "Did you recognize any of them?"

"I told you, their faces were covered," she said, mopping her tears. "If I knew who they were..." Her face darkened with anger, but her voice trailed off, as if she were afraid to finish the thought.

"I don't think they'll bother you again," Geoff reassured her. "But if you have any more trouble, you call me." He handed her his card. "This is my cell number," he pointed to the last number on the card, "in case you can't reach me at the station."

"I just don't understand why they killed my Taylor," she said, tucking his card into the pocket of her black cotton dress. "He got along just fine with white folks."

"Nobody can get along with the Klan, Jill," Geoff said, trying to keep the anger out of his voice. He got up from the sofa. "I can't promise we'll catch them, but I'm going to do my damndest to bring those bastards to justice."

She rose, too, still clutching her sodden handkerchief. "Thank you for stopping by," she said, walking him to the front door.

"You'll be in our prayers," he said. He held out his hand. After a moment, she took it, but her eyes were fixed on the dark stain that spread across the floor and onto the porch. She had scrubbed that area for an hour, but no matter what she used, the stain would not go away.

As he walked to the car, he heard the door close behind him. When he looked back at the house, he saw her shadow behind a lace-curtained window near the door.

Driving home, he thought about Jill's description of the vehicles. There had been an old, dark blue station wagon at Ken Lewis's garage. Geoff decided to drive by the shop again, and made a sharp left at the next corner.

Lewis stood in front of his shop, talking to a large, broad-shouldered man leaning against the same station wagon he had seen earlier. Hoping Lewis wouldn't notice, Geoff drove past at a normal speed, and then headed home.

The smell of roast beef and potatoes met him at the front door, and his stomach growled as he went to find his wife. Rosie was in the kitchen; her tall, slim frame covered by a red and white gingham apron over a red jersey dress. Her jet-black hair was gathered back into its usual ponytail, leaving her cheeks warm and soft, as she waited for his kiss. He walked up and caught her in a gentle embrace.

"Hey, honey, how was work today?" she asked, turning in his arms to give him a peck on the lips.

"It's been crazy," he said, pulling away to toss his uniform jacket over the back of a kitchen chair. "This Henderson murder is a mess. I stopped by to see Jill."

"I feel so badly for her and the kids. How's she doing?" Rosie asked, moving past him to open the silverware drawer. She pulled out two place settings and laid them on the counter top.

Geoff picked up the silverware and placed it on the table next to the blue-flowered dinner plates. After helping his wife put the food on the table, he sat in his chair. "She's taking it hard, but I think she'll be all right."

Coming up behind him, Rosie bent down and placed her arms around his neck. "Would you like some dessert after dinner?"

Geoff inhaled the sweet fragrance of her perfume, enjoying the warmth of her soft breasts as they pressed against him. He leaned back into her softness.

"The only dessert I want is you," he murmured.

Chapter Three

Two days after the Henderson murder, Geoff called Detective Danny Pummel, a good friend who worked undercover and was always ready to take on a new challenge.

"Hello?" Danny growled into the phone, obviously a man disturbed too early in the morning for him to pretend civility.

"Hey, Danny. It's Geoff."

There was a pause. "What the hell time is it?"

Geoff glanced at his watch. "Seven a.m."

Danny groaned again and said, "This better be good. It's my day off, and I didn't get to bed until two this morning."

"It is," Geoff said. "I want to talk to you about the Henderson murder."

"Right now?" the other man mumbled.

"Can you meet me at the Cypress Café for lunch?"

"All right" Danny sighed. "Can I go back to sleep now?"

"Sure, you bum. Next time let Connie answer the phone," Geoff laughed, hanging up.

Geoff took a shower and dressed. The delicious aroma of freshly made coffee met him as soon as he stepped into the hallway. He went downstairs with a smile on his lips.

Rosie brought him a steaming cup as soon as he sat down at the kitchen table. "So is today going to be busy?" she asked, giving him a soft kiss on the cheek.

He returned the kiss, picked up the paper, and turned to the sports section. "Yep, pretty busy," he said.

She sat down opposite him, her brow furrowed. "Promise me something?"

"Mmm," Geoff muttered, not looking up.

"Geoff!" she said sharply, causing him to look up.

He noticed tears glistening in her soft hazel eyes and was immediately contrite. "What is it, baby?"

"I need you to promise me something."

Geoff set his cup and the paper down and reached for her hand. "What is it, Rosie? Why are you so upset?"

She met his gaze, and a single tear slid down her cheek. "The Klan is nothing but a bunch of murderers. You have to promise you'll be careful, Geoff. Promise me."

He squeezed her hand. "I promise, honey. I'm always careful. You know that. I'm careful because I know you're waiting here for me, and I want us to be together until we're both old and grey. What brought this on?"

With a tremulous smile, she brushed the dampness from her wet cheek and got up to give him a longer kiss. "I love you, baby, and I worry."

He stood and folded her into his arms. "I love you, too, Rosie. Don't worry. I won't let the Klan do me in. When the time comes to take them down, I won't be doing it alone."

On his way to work, Geoff swung by Ken Lewis's garage. He noticed that the dark blue station wagon was still sitting out front. It might be worth his while to find out who it belonged to. He pulled into the drive and parked next to it.

Lewis hurried around the back of the building as Geoff got out of his car.

"Somethin' I can help you with, Lieutenant?" His expression spoke volumes, telling Geoff that he did not like nosy cops coming around.

"As a matter of fact, there is," Geoff replied, smiling. "I have a couple more questions I want to ask."

Lewis frowned. "I told you before. I don't know nothin' about no murder," he insisted, his voice rising.

"I'll decide that for myself, Ken." Geoff turned and pointed at the car sitting next to his. "Is that your station wagon?"

Lewis pushed his stringy dark hair away from his forehead, revealing beads of sweat running down his brow. "I reckon it is. Why?"

"Your station wagon fits the description of a car seen in the vicinity of the Henderson house the night of the murder." Geoff gazed at Lewis intently, trying to browbeat a confession out of him.

Lewis hesitated, as if thinking about what he could say without incriminating himself. "I'm sure I ain't the only one in this town with a blue station wagon," he said.

"You're probably right," Geoff agreed. "So why don't you tell me where you were between eleven p.m. and midnight the night before last?"

"You tryin' to blame me for that crime, Lieutenant? Cause if you are, I reckon I'd better be callin' my lawyer before I say another word."

Geoff gave Lewis credit for his attempt to look innocent, but he wasn't convinced. "If you're innocent, then you don't have anything to worry about," he answered quietly. "At the moment, I'm not trying to pin the blame on anyone, just conducting an investigation. But if you feel you need a lawyer, then maybe I had best be taking a closer look at you."

"I don't know nothin' about no murder, period. Why should I care if some colored gets himself whacked?" Lewis responded belligerently. "It's none of my business."

"I still need to know your whereabouts that night," Geoff insisted.

Lewis glared at him with murder in his eyes. "I was with the missus."

"All night?"

"What, you think I went off to get me a little piece on the side after she fell asleep?" Lewis challenged.

"What time did you go to bed?"

"After the news, my wife will vouch for me. We went to bed together and stayed that way all night."

"Mind if I confirm that with her?"

"Go right ahead," Lewis replied nonchalantly. "I ain't got nothin' to hide."

"Okay," Geoff said, "but I'll be keeping an eye on you."

He walked back to his car, his step quick and confident, convinced that Lewis and his station wagon were vital pieces to the puzzle. He knew Ken's wife would say whatever her husband wanted, so there was no point in questioning her. The man was known to knock her around from time to time, and she would do anything to avoid another beating. The Lieutenant didn't blame her, but it meant he would have to find another way to prove that Lewis was involved up to the roots of his hair.

When he arrived at the station, Geoff knocked on the Chief's door. At Waldron's abrupt command, he went in. The Chief sat at his desk, reading the newspaper and sipping coffee. The department was a small one, containing the chief, a lieutenant, a sergeant, two detectives, and ten patrol officers. It was well suited to their small town.

"Chief, I think I've got a lead on the murder."

"What do you have?" Waldron dropped his paper on the desk and motioned for the Lieutenant to sit.

Geoff dropped into the chair across from the Chief. "Yesterday evening, I stopped by the Henderson place."

"How's Mrs. Henderson doing?" the Chief asked, genuine concern in his voice.

"She's taking it real hard, but I think she'll be okay. It won't be easy, raising two kids on her own while trying to earn enough money to support them, but some of the boys and I have a couple ideas to help out, especially with T.J. And if I remember correctly, Taylor said he had a decent life insurance policy where he worked as well as a fairly substantial personal one. It should be enough, along with what she earns from Mrs. Richards to keep them out of the poor house."

"That's good to hear."

Geoff pulled a notebook from his pocket. "I asked her a few questions about the other night."

"I hope you went easy on her."

"I offered the department's condolences, as well as my own," Geoff reassured him. "I would have liked to give her a few days, possibly wait till after the funeral, but I wanted her to tell me what she remembered about that night and the cars the Klan members used, while it was still fresh in her mind."

Waldron nodded. "What did you find out?"

"She saw an old Chevy pickup truck, a red Mustang, and a dark station wagon at the scene. She wasn't certain if the wagon's color was black or blue because it was parked so that the light from the burning cross didn't reach it."

"Well, that's something, I guess," Waldron leaned forward.

"I also stopped by Ken Lewis's garage." Geoff glanced across the desk at the older man. "Oddly enough, he owns a dark blue station wagon."

Waldron's bushy white eyebrows moved upward. "We've suspected he might be involved with the Klan for some time. However, that isn't a positive I.D."

"Yeah, I know." Geoff didn't even have to think about whether or not Lewis was guilty. He was positive the man was heavily involved. "He acted guilty. Started spouting off about calling a lawyer. As far as I'm concerned, that means he's got something to hide."

The Chief nodded. "I agree. Innocent people usually don't start screaming for a lawyer. Why don't you drive Mrs.

Henderson past his shop Monday morning, and see if she can identify the vehicle."

"Okay, Chief." Geoff closed his notebook, ready to leave, but Waldron's voice stopped him.

"About that old Chevy pickup, I might know who owns it," the Chief said, "but I'm not positive."

"Who?" Geoff asked.

Waldron paused a moment. "The doctor down on Fifth Street owns one like that."

"Dr. James Corley?" Geoff said, surprised. "You think he's in the KKK?"

The Chief shrugged. "I'm not sure of anything, but it might be worth your while to check it out. Just tread very carefully with him. He's a respected member of the community and certain people won't take it kindly if they feel he's being harassed."

Geoff flipped open his notebook, scribbled the name and closed it with a snap as he stood up. "Tomorrow's Mr. Henderson's funeral," he reminded the Chief.

Waldron rose, too, his expression solemn. "I'll be there to show my respect. At a time like this, Mrs. Henderson needs to know that the community stands behind her."

As he headed out the door, Geoff stopped and looked back. "Chief, I'm meeting Danny Pummel for lunch today to discuss the case. Is that okay with you?"

The Chief reached for his hat. "It's his day off. He probably won't thank you for not waiting till he comes back on duty, but sure. Use whatever department personnel you need to break this case. Maybe the two of you can come up with something to help us stop these killings and put the Klan out of business for good... at least in this town."

"God willing," Geoff said, his face grim, "we'll figure something out."

At a quarter till noon, Geoff headed for the Cypress Café. Danny, a thirty-seven-year-old detective with blond hair and piercing blue eyes, already sat at a table drinking coffee.

"I see you made it early," Geoff greeted him.

"I see you *finally* made it, G." Danny rose to shake Geoff's hand, and then beckoned the waitress as they sat down. After Geoff ordered coffee, Danny leaned across the table and studied him for a long moment.

"So what going on, G?" Danny asked. "You sounded pretty serious on the phone."

Geoff grinned. "I'm surprised you noticed, Danny, considering I woke you from your beauty sleep."

"Aw, cut me some slack, G. This is supposed to be my day off. What's up?"

"I think I have a lead in the Henderson case." Geoff smiled. He was glad to be able to talk to someone besides the Chief about what he had discovered. "At least, it gives us somewhere to start looking."

"You think you can figure out who was involved?" Danny asked. "Because if you can, I want to help you take those bastards down."

"Why not?" Geoff smiled at the waitress when she brought his coffee, topped off Danny's cup, and took their order for burgers and fries. "Mrs. Henderson gave me a couple vehicle descriptions."

"That's not a whole lot to go on. Did anyone notice the license numbers? Any ideas about who was driving the cars?" Danny frowned when Geoff shook his head. "Well, if this was easy, I guess we wouldn't need a police department," he said wryly.

"You know how it is. Even if the neighbors saw the whole thing go down and recognized the perps, they would be too frightened to say anything."

"Got anything solid?" Danny picked up his cup and gingerly sipped the hot brew.

"No, but what else do we have to start with?" Geoff stirred cream into his cup before taking a drink.

"Well, you might think I'm crazy," Danny said, "but hear me out." He glanced around the restaurant and turned back to Geoff. "What we need is someone on the inside. Someone who blends in and can make them believe he thinks the same way they do."

Geoff frowned. "What are you getting at?"

Danny leaned forward, lowering his voice. "What if I were to join the KKK?"

Geoff's jaw dropped, and he barely noticed the waitress setting their plates in front of them. When she left, he asked, "Are you out of your mind?"

His friend picked up his hamburger and took a big bite. After chewing a few moments and then swallowing, he said, "I've been trying to uncover the KKK for years. You know that."

"I think you're nuts." Geoff shook his head. He picked up his own burger. "Wait till the Chief hears this."

Danny washed down his bite with a gulp of coffee. He carefully set the cup on the table and gazed at Geoff with serious blue eyes. "That's not what I needed to hear, G. I need you to tell me I have your support." He wiped a dab of mustard from his mouth with his napkin, adding, "If I become a member, maybe I can find out who's behind this, and we can stop them."

Silence stretched between them like a taut rubber band as they finished their meal.

Geoff knew Danny's plan made sense, but he couldn't allow his friend to place his life on the line. Still, what other choice did they have? Having someone on the inside could break the case wide open, and Danny and his German heritage fit the bill perfectly. Geoff sighed, looking across the table.

"All right, but you're going to have to be real careful and not mess up. You're putting your life on the line. If you can get the evidence we need to expose them, we can sew this case up tight. But if they figure out it was you… " Geoff left the rest of his sentence dangling.

"I know. I know. I'm dead meat, but G, what choice do we have?"

"You'll have to clear it with the Chief first."

"I won't mess up," Danny replied, his infectious grin back in place. "And *you* can tell the Chief."

"Why me?" Geoff said.

"Because you're closer to him and he listens to what you have to say," Danny said. "Although, I'm not sure we should tell him. The less people know about it, the better."

He signaled for their bill, and after the waitress brought it over, Danny pulled a few bills from his wallet and threw them on the table.

"Let's go."

Outside, they stopped next to Danny's silver Ford F-150.

"How soon are you planning to do this?" Geoff asked quietly.

"The sooner the better, Danny said, his voice tight with excitement.

Geoff frowned. "This isn't a game, you know."

Danny ran a hand through his longish blond hair, lifting it off his forehead. "I know, G. Trust me, will you?"

"All right. All right." Geoff shook his head, still trying to come to terms with his friend's idea. "How do you plan to get in?"

"Well, I reckon I'll plant a few bugs in certain people's ears and wait to see what happens." Danny glanced around before turning back to Geoff. "Believe me; someone *will* pick up on it."

"Like who?"

"Dr. Corley, for one," Danny replied.

"Dr. James Corley?" Geoff lifted an eyebrow, thinking that maybe the Chief had been right. "You think he's involved with the Klan?"

"I would bet a year's wages on it," Danny replied. "When a person works undercover, he hears all kinds of things. Things some people may not want you to know." He smiled. "If he isn't actually a member, I guarantee he knows who is."

Geoff sighed. "He's been my family doctor for years. He never seemed racist; always treated Rosie and me no differently than any of his other patients."

"That's the point, G. The smart ones never let the racism sneak out except when they're with their Klan brothers." Glancing at his watch, Danny said, "Look, I have to get going. I've got some errands to run that's going to take a couple hours. If I don't start now, I'll never make it to Corley's office in time. I want to catch him before he leaves."

Realizing his friend was determined to forge ahead, Geoff gave up. "Okay. How do you suggest we meet?"

Danny slapped Geoff's shoulder. He glanced across the bed of the pickup before opening the door. "I'll call you, but we'll have to stay under the radar." With that, he swung into the driver's seat and waved as he drove away.

Geoff walked back to his car, unease prickling the back of his neck.

At five p.m., Danny sat in his truck waiting for Dr. James Corley to come out of his downtown office. When he saw the doctor, dressed in his usual dark grey suit and white shirt, walk out the front door, he hopped out of his truck and hurried over, tucking his black Hard Rock Café t-shirt into worn Levis.

"Good evening, Dr. Corley." The doctor was an older man with a full head of white hair and cautious brown eyes. Danny reached out to shake his hand.

"I'm sorry, young man," James Corley said, a slight frown marring his haggard features as he shook Danny's hand. "I don't believe I know you."

"No, sir, you don't, but let me tell, I've heard things, and I want you to know that I agree with you one hundred percent."

The other man pulled his hand away. "One hundred percent on what?" he asked, eyeing Danny warily.

"I believe in a white America," Danny said, drawing himself to his full 5'11" height. "It's time to take back our country, don't ya think?" He purposely lengthened his drawl, making his words broad and soft.

James Corley's eyes widened and he moved away, walking hastily toward his white, late-model Cadillac. "Son, I don't have the foggiest idea what you're talking about."

Danny followed him, careful not to get too close, but anxious to make the right impression. "Well, sir, I know there are others who believe as I do, but I just don't know where to find them."

The doctor stopped at the door of the sedan and turned to face Danny, as if trying to determine the sincerity of his words. After several moments, he smiled. "Boy, you're serious, aren't you?"

"I surely am," Danny said firmly, "and I want to do my part."

"I might know someone who would be interested in speaking with you. Let me give you a number to call."

Corley reached into his briefcase and pulled out a business card and pen. He wrote a telephone number on the back of the card and handed it to Danny. "If you're serious and not just blowing smoke, call this number and follow the instructions you're given."

Danny took the card embossed with the doctor's name, office address, and phone number, and turned it over to look at the number scrawled on the back. With a grin, he tucked it inside the pocket of his jeans and offered his hand again.

James Corley shook it and smiled, revealing brilliant white teeth. "I hope you find what you're looking for, son."

When Danny arrived home at 5:30, his wife was folding laundry on the burgundy flowered living room sofa. He could smell the fresh scent of detergent and fabric softener and beneath it, the aroma of baking bread.

"Umm, it smells good in here," he said, closing the door behind him. "Come here, you."

Connie Pummel, his blonde-haired, blue-eyed wife of fifteen years stood and said, "You look awfully happy. Did you have a good day? You didn't go into to work, did you?"

He wrapped his arms around her in a bear hug. "Yes... and no, but I took care of those errands you wanted me to run."

"What did you do at work?"

"I didn't actually go into work. I met Geoff for lunch and after talking to him, I think the Henderson murder may get solved after all. If we resolve this one, we'll have a handle on the other murders and maybe stop this madness in its tracks." Danny dropped a kiss on her nose when she looked up at him.

"How?" she asked, releasing him to return to her seat on the couch.

"Geoff and I came up with a great idea on how to uncover the members of the Klan." He sat in the burgundy and brown recliner across from her.

"How?" she asked again as an anxious look slid across her face.

Gray Love

Danny knew the murders worried her. They gave her nightmares that usually ended with him being killed. Try as he might, there was nothing he could do to relieve her fears. He could have kept his cases to himself, refusing to tell her anything about them. However, Danny didn't like secrets between them, and felt that withholding knowledge of his cases would be no better than lying to her. Unfortunately, his current news wouldn't make her feel any better.

"I'm going to join the Klan," Danny announced, watching for her reaction. "You know the old saying, 'if you can't beat 'em… join 'em?'"

She dropped the socks she held and stared at him with frightened blue eyes. "Danny, are you crazy? Why would you do something like that?"

Danny left his chair to sit beside her, taking her clammy hands in his. He wanted her to understand. "Because, Connie, it's the only way I can figure out whose involved and bring them to justice."

"But what if they find out you aren't who you're pretending to be?" she asked, shuddering. "You could be killed. Then what would happen to me? How could I ever go on without you?"

He leaned over to kiss her. "Connie, you worry too much. I'll be fine."

"Oh, Danny, you and your stupid ideas," she said, her lips trembling. A tear slid down one pale cheek, landing on her pink halter top. "You think you're invincible, but you're not. One of these days, that cockiness is going to get you killed."

He put his hands on her shoulders and gave her a gentle shake. "Connie, if police officers allowed fear to rule them, we'd never catch the bad guys, and this madness would never be over." He pulled her into his arms, and whispered against her hair. "Someone has to make them stop."

Chapter Four

Taylor Henderson's funeral drew a large crowd – people from his office, friends and neighbors, and several members of the Crystal Springs Police Department. The weather was hotter than normal for spring, and the humidity was off the scale.

Henderson was to be buried in one of the few remaining plots in the small church cemetery. Row upon row of tombstones, some of which dated back a hundred and fifty years, made it difficult for the mourners to find a place to stand without bumping into one of the ancient stones. Standing near Jill Henderson Geoff kept thinking about James Corley, who had been his doctor since he was a little boy. Geoff liked him and trusted his judgment, but now he felt betrayed because the man might be part of a group that secretly hated him and others like him because of their skin color. The more he thought about it, the more he supported Danny in his attempt to unveil the society and bring its members to justice.

The sobs of Taylor Henderson's family and friends distracted Geoff as the simple coffin was lowered into the ground. Reverend Butler said the closing prayer, and Jill dropped a handful of dirt into the hole that beat a sad tattoo against the polished wooden casket. The minister offered her a hand as she left, and she thanked him profusely for his kind words about her husband. Jill's two children clung to her black skirt as she headed for the waiting limo.

Geoff walked Chief Waldron to his Ford Crown Victoria, and climbed into the passenger seat so he could speak to him in private about Danny's idea.

Waldron looked at him expectantly, holding his keys in his hand.

"We might be closer to solving this murder than I thought, Chief" Geoff said in a quiet voice.

Waldron took a deep breath. "How?" he asked. "Have you received another lead?"

"No, but Danny has a plan that is going to break the case wide open." Geoff glanced through the windows at the area surrounding the vehicle, making sure no one came close. He needed to be certain that only the Chief heard his next quiet words. "He's going to join the Klan."

"Join the KKK? That's nonsense." The Chief's keys fell from his hand and onto the floor of the car, but he didn't seem to notice. "What if they find out he's a mole?"

"We'll deal with it." Geoff shrugged. "Think about it, Chief. You've been trying to figure out who they are for years. As long as we're in the dark about the members' identity, we'll never be able to bring them to justice."

Waldron nodded, but he didn't look happy. "That's true," he conceded. "However, I don't like placing Danny in such a dangerous position."

"This is the only way we'll ever be able find who belongs to the organization." Geoff glanced around again and brought his gaze back to his boss's concerned face. "You know what I'm saying is true."

"I just think the two of you should be careful, that's all," Waldron said gruffly. "I don't want to see any of my people hurt."

"We'll be careful," Geoff said.

As Geoff got out of the car, Waldron added, "One more thing."

Geoff leaned back in for a moment, meeting the Chief's serious blue eyes with a smile. "Chief, you always have 'one more thing.' What's this one?"

The older man smiled at Geoff's comment. "I just wanted to say good luck. Both of you make me mighty proud."

* * *

Sitting in his office at home, Danny stared at the card in his hand, and finally flipped his cell phone open to dial the number written on the back.

A man, whose voice he did not recognize, answered. "Yes?"

"My name is Danny Pummel." Danny gripped the phone tightly, trying to sound casual and Southern. "I got this number from a man named James Corley."

There was a long pause. He frowned. Maybe he had dialed the wrong number; maybe he had already said something to tip the man off. This whole thing could turn out to be the biggest mistake of his career. No, more than that... his life.

"How can I help you?" The man on the phone sounded detached, and Danny shifted uncomfortably, wondering how this would go down if he played it wrong.

"I'm interested in joining your organization." Danny went for cool and not too eager.

"What organization would that be?"

Danny took a deep breath. "I'm a police detective, and I want to join the KKK." Danny filled his voice with fake conviction.

"A detective?" the other man said. "That's very interesting. Providing I knew anything about the KKK, why would someone like you want to join? You're one of the people trying to put the Klansmen in prison."

"Listen, sir," Danny said, his tone harsh, "the kind of work I do has opened my eyes to what's going on. I'm tired of colored folk blaming their problems on racism and white people, while they commit crimes and expect to get off because we have racially profiled them." He added a touch of sarcasm to the words.

A chuckle told him he had hit the mark.

"So what are you going to do about it, son?" The question came quick and probing.

"I've had enough, sir," Danny answered fiercely. "I want to stand up against them. I want to show them we're not going to take their crap any longer."

Silence reigned for several beats, before the man spoke again. "All right, calm down, Danny; I hear you. We need to talk. Can you come to my house out on Knick Road tomorrow night?"

Knick Road, Danny thought. *Wow, this guy lives in the rich part of town.* The detective pulled his notepad over and picked up a pen. "Yes, sir," he said. "Give me an address and time, and I'll be there."

The voice on the other end of the line gave him the information he needed to meet with him the following night.

"I'll see you at seven, sir," Danny said, ready to hang up.

The voice stopped him. "Oh and Danny… one more thing."

"What's that?" Danny picked up the pen he had just set down.

"Don't tell a soul," the voice ordered. "If I find out you're stringing me…

Danny smiled. "I'm not stringing you, sir. I swear. See you tomorrow. Thanks so much."

He punched the off button on his phone and tore the page off his notepad, folding it carefully before slipping it and his phone into his jacket pocket. Tomorrow night, things would start rolling. Now all he had to do was break the news to Connie.

Chapter Five

Sunday morning, approximately twelve hundred parishioners gathered in the beautiful brick church that housed the *Faith in Light Ministry*. Reverend Charles Butler gracefully stood before the mixed-race congregation, smiling down at them with no hint of prejudice. The stout, forty-five-year-old, was five-feet-eight inches tall with medium brown hair that was beginning to grey at the temples. A confirmed bachelor, who primarily focused on his church and its members, he commanded the respect of both his congregation and the community in general.

After the services were over, Reverend Butler went into his paneled study and planned the KKK's budget report for their next meeting, which would take place that night. The Klan budgeted money for firearms and wood and as treasurer, he made sure they were well prepared for any situation, keeping the supplies hidden in a small room, located in the basement of the church. At twelve-thirty that afternoon, his phone rang.

"Charlie, it's me." James Corley didn't even bother to say hello.

The Reverend smiled, amused by Corley's officious tone. "Good afternoon, James. What can I do for you?"

"I wanted to let you know we have a visitor coming to tonight's meeting. I've checked him out and didn't find anything derogatory. If the guy is legit, he could be a very valuable member." Corley sounded like he expected an argument.

"That's fine," Reverend Butler said as he carefully wrote each figure on his budget sheet, including the latest shipment of wood. "Did you need me to do something, or should I just warn everyone to play it close?"

A snort sounded across the line. "They'll know not to blurt out anything important. I just wanted to let you know, because I want to bring up recruiting, before he arrives. We need more believers."

"Finding believers is my business," the Reverend laughed. "I think we're doing just fine, but we can discuss it if you like."

"I told him to come a half hour after the meeting starts."

Charles Butler smiled. "Okay. I'll see you tomorrow, James."

* * *

At six-thirty on Sunday evening, Geoff called Danny to see if he'd had any luck. "Did you find anything?"

"You could at least say hi, G." Danny's grin came across the air waves along with his words. "Hey, you wouldn't believe who I'm going to see tonight."

"Who?"

"Judge Mathew Stephens," Danny replied after a dramatic pause.

"Really? Did he tell you who he was?"

"Not a peep, but I checked the address he gave me for the meeting," Danny said. "Guess he's not too worried about my finding out who he is."

"I knew it," Geoff said, slapping his hand against the top of the kitchen table. "I can't help wondering just how many of our so-called esteemed citizens are members as well."

"I'm going to see the judge tonight," Danny answered. "Maybe even meet a few of the Klan members."

"Wow! That was fast."

"I told Corley I'm a cop."

"Was that wise?" Geoff asked, sounding worried.

"Sooner or later they were bound to find out. I figured it would be better to tell them right from the beginning. Otherwise, they might realize that I'm working undercover, but if I let them know everything up front, they won't panic when they check me out."

Geoff frowned. As far as he was concerned, things were moving a little too fast, but that was probably what they needed. "Makes sense," he said. "Just be careful."

"I will," Danny promised. "I'd better get going, okay?"

"Sure," Geoff replied. "Call me when you get back."

As he hung up the phone, Geoff wished he could go and cover Danny's back, but Danny was a good cop. He would be all right. Subconsciously, Geoff crossed his fingers, just like he used to do when he was a kid.

As Danny drove to the meeting, he tried to control his anxiety. This was the case of a lifetime, and he sure as hell didn't want to blow it. It also was the first time he had ever visited Judge Stephens' home, an impressive Victorian with a gingerbread wrap-around porch. He drove down the driveway, lined with stately Autumn Blaze Maple trees and parked next to a pickup that matched the description Jill Henderson had given Geoff.

Luke Fields, an elderly man with gray hair and matching eyes, answered the door, assessing Danny carefully. After a moment or two, he opened the heavy wooden door wide.

"You must be Danny Pummel," he said, offering a hand. "Everyone's been talking about you wanting to join our little group. Come on in."

"Thank you, sir," Danny replied, gripping the other man's hand firmly.

He followed Fields into a room filled with men and books, an old-fashioned library complete with leather chairs, brandy, and cigar smoke. Several members were gathered around the fireplace, holding drinks and cigars, chatting amiably among themselves.

"Welcome, Danny." A handsome man of about fifty stepped forward and offered his hand in greeting. Dressed in a blue Oxford shirt and khakis, he stood a head taller than the Detective. "I'm Judge Mathew Stephens."

"Nice to meet you, Judge Stephens," Danny replied, returning the handshake.

"Have a seat over there on the couch." He waved Danny toward an open space on the burgundy leather sofa. "I've got beer in the fridge, or perhaps something a little stronger, if you like."

"No, thank you, sir," Danny replied. "I'm fine."

"Not on duty, I hope," Mathew laughed.

Danny smiled and shook his head no.

"Sorry, just a little joke, let's get started."

Danny sat down, schooling his expression into one of interest to hide the shock he felt by the identities of the men around him. To his right was Dean Frances, owner of Frances Lunch and Deli Shop. Next to Dean was Howard Young, a mid-thirties stockbroker who worked in the same office as Taylor Henderson. He probably was the one who had fingered Taylor to his cronies. Danny wondered if Young had wanted Henderson's promotion and set him so that the Klan could remove him from the picture. Geoff had mentioned that, according to rumors circulating around the firm, Young was favored as Henderson's replacement. Standing near the fireplace was Robert Hemming, a clerk at the courthouse, and Bobby Robichaux, the local barber.

Danny was dumbfounded to see Reverend Charles Butler to his left, casually dressed in black pants and a light blue shirt. His collar was like a slap in God's face, defying the commandments *Thou Shall not Kill and Love Thy Neighbor.*

Ken Lewis sat next to Reverend Butler, a beer halfway to his mouth. The last two were strangers to Danny. He would later learn that their names were Chris Thibodaux and Sky Frances, Dean's younger brother.

"Thank you all for coming," Mathew said. "I'd like to introduce Danny Pummel."

Danny acknowledged their greetings with a nod.

"Danny's a local detective here in Crystal Springs, who has seen firsthand, the crimes and atrocities committed by the coloreds. I feel he would be a great addition, because he has access to areas of the law we may need in order to move forward."

The Judge gave Danny a fatherly smile before continuing. "You will need to attend four meetings before officially becoming a member."

The Detective nodded, making a mental note of everyone in the room while the Judge continued. Danny looked at each face in turn, wondering what they were doing in the middle of an organization that killed people they didn't like just to make a point – racism at its finest.

"We're here tonight because we believe that white men have the right to be free of blacks, who seem to have taken over our country, sabotaging our jobs and livelihoods, even our politics," Judge Stephens said, drawing himself to his full six feet to address the group. "We have a right to feel safe and secure in our homes, and we shouldn't have to tolerate gangs and gangstas made up of illiterate blacks too lazy to work," he spat distastefully. "It's time we put them in their place. White folks should not have to listen to the sound of ghetto music. It's ugly and filled with foul suggestions that poison our children's minds. Why hell, it can't even be called music, just some stupid guy talking in rhyme to a beat. No real talent there."

Danny shifted in his chair, suddenly uncomfortable with what he was hearing, but he knew he had to play along so as not to arouse suspicion. The men around him stirred, heads nodding and whispered assents fluttering around the room. Danny followed suit.

"These niggers need to be taught a lesson," he continued, raising his fist in the air. "And who better to teach them than the sons of Almighty God, the fairest of the human race? We are those men."

He ended his speech with a flourish, raising his voice to echo back from every corner of the large room. Several of the men jumped to their feet, echoing his gesture of militant freedom, fisted hands raised.

Danny nodded and forced his expression into a determined, agreeable look as he watched and fought back the nausea that threatened to overwhelm him, unable to believe such views still existed, but he raised his fist, too.

"We need to work on our next mission," Mathew continued. "Our new target is a man named Charlie Collins, the owner of Charlie's Bakery."

A murmur went through the room.

"What's Collins been doing?" Luke Fields asked. "He always towed the line in the past, for the most part."

"He's been opening his mouth about who he thinks our members are," Mathew growled. "A week from this Wednesday, we'll show him God's plan. We'll burn his bakery first, then ride out to his house and show him the true light of the cross. But this time, I don't want anybody doing any shooting. Is that clear? We don't need any more dead bodies riling up the police."

"I heard his daughter's a lawyer in Jackson," Luke said, looking a bit nervous.

"That doesn't matter; he needs to be taught a lesson," Mathew replied with an easy smile. He barely waited for the vocalized assent before he went on. "Now, let's discuss our budget. Charlie, where do we stand, money-wise?"

The Reverend stepped forward and read aloud from the papers in his hand. "We've got a budget of five thousand dollars. It's dues time again for you official members. That money goes to the buy the supplies we need for our work."

Danny looked on as the members formed a line in front of Charles. When Luke Fields finished paying, he walked back and took a seat next to Danny. "So, Danny, what do you think of our meeting so far?"

"I'm excited to be here," Danny replied, "and anxious to become an official member."

"Good for you," Luke nodded, grinning. "We could use more fine upstanding young men such as yourself."

After they returned to their seats, Mathew addressed the members once more. "This meeting is adjourned. Remember, our next get-together will be a week from today at 8:00 p.m. We'll gather here again. It will be an important one, so don't forget."

There was a flurry of movement as everyone headed toward the door.

When Danny stood, Mathew called him over. "Hey, Danny, I'd like to speak with you a moment before you leave."

Danny paused, turning to where the judge leaned against the carved marble fireplace. He stood with one hand tucked into his pants pocket, the picture of Southern gentility.

"Yes, sir?" Danny walked over to the older man, feeling the beginning of a nervous sweat. Did they suspect him already? It seemed like they had accepted him almost too easily.

"What did you think of what we had to say?"

Danny smiled, resisting the urge to wipe his brow. He just had to appear calm, and everything would be fine. "I agree 100% and can't wait till the next meeting." He kept his voice calm, cautiously enthusiastic.

The other man straightened and stepped closer, dropping an arm across Danny's shoulders. "So you still want to join?"

It looked like they were going to let him in, as long as he didn't blow it. "Of course I do. I'm surprised by the members you have – some of the finest men in our fair city. I am honored to become a part of your organization."

Mathew smiled and slapped him on the back as they walked toward the front door. "This is an honorable society, son. Be proud of who you are. We represent white American pride. There's nothing wrong with wanting to be separate from the coloreds and other infidels in the world. Even the Bible supports us."

He stopped just short of the entrance and offered his hand. "We are doing God's work, son, lending a helping hand, you could say. Join us and you will be blessed."

"I will, Judge Stephens," Danny said with a proud smile. "Thank you for giving me this opportunity."

Danny shook Mathew's hand and headed for his truck, thinking about the meeting and its members. In two short hours, his whole life had changed. As he turned the key, he watched the taillights of the departing cars, and shook his head. Many of those men were community leaders he had once respected. People he had never imagined could commit such foul atrocities.

As soon as he got home, Danny retrieved his Wireless RF Signal Detector that he used to locate hidden bugs and cameras and carefully checked every room of the house. He had purchased the device with his own money, because the police department's budget did not have a lot of funds for extras. The

Detective figured he could use it as a tax deduction, but more importantly, it was a vital piece of equipment that had saved him from blowing his cover on more than one occasion.

Danny suspected that sometime, when he and his wife were both away from home, the Klan might take the opportunity to plant a few bugs and listen in to make sure his views at home were the same as the ones he expressed at the meeting. Connie had been at Bible study for part of the evening, and he did not want to take any chances. If they had bugged the house, he wanted to know about it. After assuring himself that the place was clean, he called Geoff, using a throwaway cell phone. The number he punched in was for another throwaway the Lieutenant kept for occasions such as these. Neither man dared to use his regular cell or their personal land lines. It might be illegal for ordinary citizens to tap a phone line, but that never kept the determined ones from doing it, and he believed that over the next four weeks, the Klan would be carefully listening to everything he had to say.

After two rings, Geoff answered the phone.

"That you, Danny?"

"Hey, I made it back and have an official invitation to join the KKK. You wouldn't believe who attended tonight."

"Who?" Geoff asked, grabbing a pen and his trusty notebook.

"Mathew Stephens is their leader," Danny answered, still unable to believe it. He heard the sound of Geoff's pen scratching against paper as he wrote.

"Who else?" Geoff asked.

Danny recited the list of names he had memorized, feeling nausea rise in his throat once more as he thought about these men committing murder – men he had once believed were law abiding citizens.

"You mean to tell me that Reverend Butler is also involved in this?" Geoff asked incredulously. "And I eat at Dean Frances's deli at least three times a week."

"Yeah, I know. By the way, they have more cross burnings planned. Charlie Collins is next on the list." Danny frowned, looking up to see Connie standing in the kitchen doorway, her hand covering her mouth and a horrified expression on her face. He motioned her to sit while he finished his conversation.

"Are you sure about that?" Geoff asked. "We have to warn him."

"I'm positive. I'll find out the details and let you know, but we have to be careful how we handle this. If the Klan discovers that its intended targets are suddenly being warned, they'll know I'm the one doing it," he said, glancing over at his wife. "They'll be meeting again next Sunday at eight p.m."

"I can't believe it," Geoff growled into the phone. "I'll let Chief Waldron know first thing in the morning."

"Fine," Danny agreed, "Just remember, we can't let this information leak out, or it'll blow my cover for sure."

"I know, but I have to warn Charlie so he can figure out what he wants to do." Geoff sounded tired and dispirited, and Danny hated hearing that sound in his friend's voice.

"You do that. Take care. I'll call as soon as I have more information," Danny said. "We'll have to be very careful we're not seen together outside of work until this is over. The last thing I want them to learn is that we're friends. It could bring a lot of hurt down on you and your family."

"It might be a good idea if you let some disgust creep into your expression and voice whenever we're seen together in public."

"Except for when we're in the presence of the other officers; I don't want them wondering what's going on. If they spoke of it outside the precinct, and the right person got wind of the change in our relationship, the difference in attitude might trigger even more suspicions. This way if asked, I can say that I have to hide it at work because you're my superior," Danny concluded.

"Danny boy, I'm proud of you." Geoff's praise came quietly. "You take care of yourself."

Danny hung up the phone and walked to where Connie was huddled in the chair opposite him. He drew her up and enfolded her in a comforting embrace, whispering soft words of love against her cheek.

After a few moments, she pushed him away. "Tell me you're not going back, Danny," she demanded, fear in her eyes.

He looked down at her and sighed. "I'm sorry. I can't promise that, sweetheart. This is something I have to do. They gave me a number to call, and I went to a meeting tonight," he said, gently wiping her face with his fingers. "I found out who's in charge."

Connie pushed his hand away, looked up and asked. "Who? Who is the monster leading that pack of rabid mongrels?"

"Mathew Stephens."

"The judge?" She was as shocked as if he had just told her that the President of the United States was a Chinese Communist.

Danny nodded. "Can you believe it?"

"Oh, my God, Danny," she whispered. "You can't go after someone like him. The man's too powerful. You'll be murdered for sure." Connie stepped back, left the room, and stood at the kitchen sink, but even at this distance, he could see that her lips were trembling.

"You can't do this to me, Danny," she said angrily, her hands clenching into fists. "I do not want to open my door some day to find one of your police friends on the doorstep, telling me you're dead."

Gray Love

He moved toward her, but she held up her hand, and he stopped. He didn't know how to explain how his world was falling apart, now that he knew that some of the people he had thought of as friends were actually enemies of everything he believed to be right and just. He needed her to be there for him, but at the same time, realized that he had to be there for her, too.

"Connie, I'll promise you this," he declared, his voice confident. "I will make it through this, and I will stop these men from murdering anyone else." He looked at her, pleadingly. "I have to do this, for the people who have already died, and those who are yet to become victims of these madmen. Somebody has to stop them, and I have the right color of skin to do it. Besides, I can't back out now. It would cause too much suspicion."

Connie stared at him, tears filling her blue eyes, as she ran to him and wrapped her arms around his chest, squeezing tight.

Danny tightened his arms around her, murmuring against her soft blonde hair, "It's going to be all right."

In his heart, he hoped it would be.

Chapter Six

"Good morning, Hannah. I just brewed a fresh pot of coffee. Want a cup?" Deborah Collins asked as she stirred scrambled eggs in a pan on the stove.

"No, Ma. I'm fine," Hannah answered, sitting down at the table tucked into the breakfast nook of the large kitchen. "I'm trying to limit my caffeine intake."

The older woman turned to look at her daughter, her brown eyes showing surprise. "Since when, girl?"

"Since now," Hannah jokingly replied as she picked up her napkin and deposited it in her lap. "I hate Mondays, and the knuckleheads I deal with only make it worse."

"Your father and I sent you to a good school so you could make something of yourself. Now you get paid decent money to deal with those kinds of people," her mother said, dishing up the food. She set a plate of grilled ham, eggs and toast in front of Hannah. "You sure look nice in that new blue suit, very professional."

"Thanks, Ma." Hannah sighed, reaching for her fork. She took a bite of eggs, and smiled at her mother, noticing how pretty she looked this morning. Her gray hair was caught up in a bun at the back of her neck with feathery tendrils stroking her high cheek bones. She touched her own dark hair, smoothed back into a business-like chignon.

"That Williams boy called for you last night." Her mother brought her own plate of food to the table and sat down.

"Kenneth?" Hannah paused with a forkful of eggs halfway to her mouth and grimaced.

"He's prying cause, he fancies you," her mother gently rebuked. "Kenneth is a fine young man. Someday, he's gonna be famous with that guitar of his."

Hannah rolled her eyes. "Yeah, one day, Ma, and I won't care a bit when he does." Setting down her fork, she placed the remaining ham and eggs on a piece of toast, folding it in half. Standing up, she grabbed her briefcase and headed for the kitchen door. "I'll eat this in the car. I gotta go. Bye, Ma. Give Daddy a kiss for me."

As she approached her black Maxima, Geoff Tray pulled in the driveway and got out of his car.

"Good morning, Miss Collins," he greeted her.

She smiled as he approached. "Good morning, Geoff. How's Rosie?"

"She's doing just fine, ma'am," he replied. "Is your father home?"

"He is." She motioned toward the back door before getting into her car and starting it. Monday was *not* a good day to be late.

Putting the car in gear, Hannah glanced at the kitchen window before backing out of the drive. Through the parted lace curtains, she saw her mother speaking to Lieutenant Tray. She smiled. *Mom is probably trying to get him to eat something while he waits for Dad to get out of the shower,* she thought.

Frowning, she wondered what Geoff wanted with her father. She hoped there hadn't been any trouble at the bakery. With that thought came another, more serious one, regarding the recent murders. Hannah dealt with criminals and the law every day, but if she ever found out who shot and killed Taylor Henderson and the elderly Mr. King, who had been murdered a couple weeks earlier, she would be sorely tempted to shoot the bastards herself. This was the twenty-first century for crying out loud. Didn't they know that racism and hate were dying and on the way out in the United States? Yes, it still existed to a small degree, especially in some of the elderly. But racism was a heck of a lot deader than it had been fifty years ago. At any rate, she didn't have time to worry about it now. She was late for work.

Inside the Collins house, Geoff greeted Deborah Collins as she bustled about the kitchen, preparing breakfast for her husband.

"I hope nothing's wrong, Geoff," she said, smoothing her hands on her embroidered apron. "Would you like some breakfast?"

He smiled at her reassuringly. "No, ma'am, Rosie fed me before I left, but I need to talk to your husband before he leaves for work."

"Is something wrong at the bakery? Did we have a break-in or something?"

"No, ma'am, the bakery is fine."

Deborah sighed with relief and went to the bottom of the wide stairs that led to the bedrooms above. "Charlie, are you out of the shower yet? Geoff Tray is here to speak with you," she called. She led the Lieutenant into the living room, motioning him to take a seat on the chintz couch as she perched on the arm of a matching chair, folding her hands in her lap. "What brings you out this way?"

Geoff leaned forward, elbows on his knees, fingers twined together. After a deep breath, he said, "I have some information about the Klan."

Her face fell, making her look older than her sixty-two years. "Oh my, I hope they aren't planning more trouble."

Geoff opened his mouth, but before he could say anything further, Charlie Collins walked in with his hand extended. The Lieutenant rose and shook it. With a nod, he sat again, and Charlie settled himself into the chair his wife had vacated as she headed for the kitchen.

With his short, curly gray hair still damp from the shower, Charlie Collins gave Geoff an inquisitive look. The Lieutenant had known the family since he was a boy. Charlie had coached his little league team. The man looked much older now, his sturdy body a bit heavier, and his movements a tad slower.

Charlie's eyes glittered with intelligence. "What brings you out here this morning?"

There really wasn't a good way to say it, so Geoff took a deep breath and said, "Mr. Collins, I've come this morning to warn you about the KKK." He looked directly into the older man's hazel eyes. "They're targeting you and your bakery, and it's going to be soon."

A crash made both men turn around. Deborah stood in the doorway, a plate of ham, eggs and toast broken into a mess at her feet.

"What?" she asked, her face turning a sickly pale shade. "What did you say? Why us? We mind our own business and never bother anybody."

"I've had that bakery for fifty years. They never objected to it before. Why now?" Charlie asked.

Geoff jumped to his feet and hurried over to Deborah, taking her arm and gently guiding her to the sofa. "I'm sorry to break it to you so bluntly, but according to my informant, they plan to burn the bakery, and then come here." He returned to the kitchen doorway and knelt down to clean up the mess.

"Are you sure?" Charlie asked.

"I wish I could say no… that it was only speculation, but my informant said they are planning to do it a week from Wednesday," Geoff replied reluctantly.

"Who are these people?" Anger and fear warred in the older man's voice.

Geoff glanced at him, realizing that Charlie was looking for answers he did not have. "We don't really know, but we're hoping to find out very soon," he told Charlie. "In the meantime, I'm going to arrange for police surveillance on the shop and protection for your family."

"But I have to work. I can't just close up the business and hide in a corner. I have a responsibility to my employees and my clients, and what about my daughter? How am I supposed to protect her?" Charlie's eyes moistened. His wife hurried to his side, settling on the arm of the chair once more as she slid an arm behind him and rubbed his back. He patted her leg absentmindedly.

"I'll be checking on Hannah at the courthouse," Geoff said, "the rest of the time, be careful and keep your eyes open, okay?"

His expression troubled, the older man nodded. "I don't understand why they would do such a thing."

Geoff didn't know what to tell him, or how to promise Charlie that things wouldn't get out of hand, but it was the best he could do for now. "I don't understand either, but we needed to warn you and offer some kind of protection."

"I can't listen to this," Deborah said. Taking the broken plate and food debris from Geoff's hands and heading into the kitchen.

Charlie nodded, still frowning. "Thanks, Geoff." He stood up. "I'll be damned before I let them burn down everything I've worked so hard for," he said defiantly.

Geoff brushed his hands together. "Please tell Hannah to be careful as well." He held out his hand.

Charlie stood and firmly shook the Lieutenant hand.

"We certainly will," Mrs. Collins said, standing in the kitchen doorway once more. "I'm not going to let anyone harm our baby."

"Good," Geoff said, smiling. "I'll be back to check on you. I have to head over to the station and talk to the Chief."

Charlie walked him to the door. "You take care now, Geoff, and thanks."

"One more thing, Mr. Collins."

"What's that?"

"I have to ask you and your family to keep this under your hat. Don't say a word to anyone about this or let anyone know about the precautions you'll be taking. A man's life depends on it."

"Don't you worry, Lieutenant, we won't say anything to anyone except Hannah, and when I explain the need for secrecy, she'll keep quiet about it, too."

"Thank you, sir."

Geoff returned to his car, raising a hand in farewell to the couple before heading downtown. At the station, he barely took enough time to stop by his desk and check his messages before hurrying into Chief Waldron's office.

"Chief?"

"Well, good morning to you, too," the older man replied with a hint of sarcasm, looking up from the paperwork on his desk. "Every time I see you, you're in a hurry, Geoff. What's gone and lit a fire under your rear end this time?"

"Sorry, Chief. Good morning," Geoff said, seating himself in the hard wooden chair in front of Waldron's desk. "You won't believe the latest." He pulled his pad out of his shirt pocket, and flipped it open before looking across the desk at the other man. "Danny stopped by Dr. Corley's office at closing time on Friday."

"Really? Went right to the source, did he?" The Chief raised an eyebrow. "How did he approach him?"

"Danny kinda felt him out with a few appropriate remarks. At first, Corley played dumb, but eventually, he gave him a business card with a phone number on the back. Danny went home and called the number right away," Geoff said.

"And?"

"He went to a KKK meeting last night."

"Hmm," the Chief murmured, looking thoughtful. "So he's really serious about this?"

"You bet he is."

Waldron nodded, his bright blue gaze was inquisitive. "What did he find out?"

"The meeting was at the home of Mathew Stephens, who is the head of the whole thing," Geoff said.

"You mean our Judge Mathew Stephens?" Waldron looked incredulous as he drummed the end of his pencil on his desk.

"The same," Geoff said, "and there's more."

The Chief leaned back in his chair expectantly.

"James Corley, Dean Frances, and Luke Fields are also involved, to name a few."

The Chief sat up straight. "Wow, you boys did a great job getting names so quickly."

Geoff grimaced. "And who is the pastor of your church?"

"Reverend Charles Butler," the older man slowly replied, his eyes narrowing. "Why?"

"Well, you can add him to the list, as well," Geoff said. "He's the treasurer."

"Well I'll be damned," Waldron said, opening his notebook and licking the end of his pencil before proceeding to write. He paused and stared at Geoff. "These are all respected men of the community. I'm shocked to say the least. It won't be easy taking them down, especially the judge. Anything else?"

The Lieutenant gave him the rest of the names and said, "Yes. They're planning their next attack against Charlie Collins and his bakery."

"If we want to make a good case, we almost have to catch them at the scene of the crime." The Chief laid his pencil down. "Any suggestions?"

"Until Danny goes to the next meeting, we won't know anything more," Geoff said, rolling an idea around in his head. "Maybe we should arrest them at their next meeting. Danny could wear a wire and once they've incriminated themselves..."

Chief Waldron frowned. "You know better than that, Geoff. It's a free country. We can't arrest them for going to a meeting, even if it is the Klan. We need proof. Besides, it's too easy to detect a wire these days, even though some of them are as small as a button or made up to look like a pen or some other inconspicuous item. There's plenty of money in that group. I wouldn't put it past them to have bug detectors in place to check their members, especially the new ones. Why some of them detecting gizmos are as small as a cell phone. One of them could put it in his pocket, and set it to go off silently if it detects something. If they suspect Danny of wearing a bug, they wouldn't think twice about killing him and dumping the body in the swamps for gator food."

"We could expose them in the newspapers," Geoff suggested. "Let people know who they are. It would make it pretty difficult for them to operate. Their operation relies on secrecy. Take that away, and it would be like pulling the teeth on a bobcat."

Waldron looked up. "It's too soon. A leak to the paper would practically scream that we're on to them. Maybe it would shut them down, or maybe they would just get a few Klan members from another area to handle things for them. Either way, I want to do more than just stop them. I want them to pay for killing those innocent men."

"So do I, Chief. Finding enough evidence to put them away for those murders is going to be difficult, unless we can nail the weakest link and get him to rat out the others."

"I wouldn't hold my breath. Let's just see what Danny finds out at the next meeting before we make any plans on how to take them down."

Geoff turned to go, but stopped. "Chief?"

"Yeah?" The older man glanced up again, still frowning.

"The Collins family is going to need protection. The Klan isn't supposed to go after them until a week from Wednesday, but you never can tell." Geoff held up two fingers. "Two units ought to do."

"Thing is, if the Klan sees we're providing protection, they're gonna suspect that Danny spilled the beans."

"I don't want anything happening to Danny, but we can't allow those murdering bastards to destroy the Collins' livelihood and possibly their lives, too, Chief. Now that we know what the Klan is planning, we have to take measures to protect these folks."

"I realize that. I just don't know how we're going to pull it off without blowing Danny's cover. I'll think of something. I'm not allowing another decent family to become victims if I can help it."

"What are you going to do?"

Without answering, the Chief picked up the phone.

Chapter Seven

Hannah Collins decided to stop by the Tiger Lounge for a late lunch. It was an upscale night club that, even at this early hour, was fairly packed with customers, looking for good music to listen to as they enjoyed a tasty lunch. A corner-shaped bar made of beach wood, with matching vertical barstools that had upholstered seats in burnt orange, occupied the left front corner of the room. Round beach wood tables, chairs, and booths took up two-thirds of the room, and the remaining area was filled with a stage, centered against the back wall with flashy lighting and décor, and a dance floor.

With a cheeseburger on order and a glass of cold lemonade in front of her, Hannah's day didn't seem quite so bad.

Kenneth Williams, the local musician her mother kept trying to fix her up with, spotted her and carried his drink from the bar to join her.

"What brings you here, Hannah?" Kenneth pulled out a chair and sat down without an invitation. He was casually dressed in the half-buttoned black silk shirt and black leather pants he had made his signature outfit.

"Hi, Ken," she said, studying his handsome features. She felt he was almost too pretty to be a man.

"You look absolutely beautiful this afternoon," he said, flashing perfectly even white teeth.

"Thank you," she said demurely, lowering her eyes. She took a sip of lemonade, wondering if he expected her to return the compliment as she set her drink down and patted her lips with a napkin.

"Are you busy Friday evening?" he asked, leaning forward, elbows on the table.

"Why?" She dreaded his next question.

"Well," he said, "I was wondering if you would like to go out to dinner with me."

"Kenneth," she began, but couldn't think of an excuse she hadn't already used a hundred times. Inwardly, she sighed in resignation. "Sure, I'd love to go out with you."

He grinned from ear to ear, looking like a man who had just won the lottery. "Great! I'll pick you up at seven-thirty."

"Okay," she replied, and then smiled a "thank you" to the waitress who had just brought her burger.

Kenneth slid to his feet gracefully and touched her shoulder. "I have to get back to playing before the lounge fires me."

She watched him saunter back on stage. As she took a bite of the thick juicy burger with everything but onions on it, Kenneth picked up the microphone and looked directly at her. "This next song is dedicated to the most beautiful woman I know."

Hannah felt her cheeks flush as he began singing *When a Man Loves a Woman*.

While he sang, he looked directly at her. Hannah allowed the blissful tune fill her soul, wondering why she couldn't fall in love with him. He was everything she should have wanted in a man. Why couldn't she just accept it? Knowing she didn't have an answer, she left her partially eaten sandwich and enough money to cover the bill plus a tip on the table and made a hasty escape, giving him a brief nod of acknowledgement as she headed for the door.

It was a quarter to two, but she really didn't want to go back to the office. Mondays always wore her out. Instead, she drove to a small nearby lake situated off Knick Road. A nice, refreshing swim might help her feel like her life wasn't totally off track.

* * *

Mathew Stephens left his office early to go fishing. He stopped by his house to change into faded blue jeans and a light blue cotton shirt that had seen better days. Gathering his fishing equipment, he headed outside. The hot afternoon sun cast a shadow before him as he crossed the garden behind his home, complete with several species of beautiful roses, hand-crafted, white cedar, lattice-work arbors, trellises, and a gazebo, partially shaded by magnolia and pecan trees. Leaving the garden he walked across the manicured lawn, and then followed a well-worn path through a field toward the lake, where he and his grandfather used to fish.

Bees buzzed lazily in the June heat, tasting the sweet nectar of wildflowers and Black-eyed Susan's as they flew along the path he had chosen. He waved one away as it flew near his face, pulled a beat-up ball cap from his back pocket, and settled it firmly on his head. Long before he reached the lake, his shirt grew damp and clung to his skin, and sweat stung his eyes.

As he approached the mangrove and long needled pine trees that surrounded the lake like tall sentinels, he heard splashing, and stopped just out of sight to see who was trespassing on his property. He caught his breath when he saw a naked woman swimming lazily through the opaque water, her dark hair floating behind her. Dark blue clothing along with lacy white under things hung from a nearby brush, and he felt a tightening in his body, wondering what the silky chemise would feel like against her skin. It had been too long since he had been in a committed relationship, too long since Cynthia Burkhart had broken his heart, and his body missed the benefits of such a commitment.

He stood behind a tree and watched her move gracefully through the water, her limbs sliding through the lake like chocolate syrup through milk. God, she was beautiful. A moment later, she climbed out and began wringing the water out of her long dark hair. Mathew eyes widened at the lovely shape of her body. Her mocha-colored skin glistened enticingly. It wasn't until that moment that he realized she was black. Despite that recognition, his body responded in ways he had almost forgotten.

She pulled on her panties, having difficulty because of her wet skin, and reached for the delicate chemise, hanging next to what looked like a blue business suit. Unknowingly, he must have moved or possibly sighed too loudly, because her eyes came up quickly, and she gave a small cry before reaching for her tailored white blouse. She quickly buttoned her shirt and turned away, trying to wriggle into her skirt.

"Didn't your mama teach you any manners?" With her skirt safely zipped, she turned and glared at him, holding the remaining piece of clothing, a jacket that matched the skirt, like a shield in front of her.

"You're trespassing on private property." He grinned mischievously. "There's nothing wrong with watching a woman, if she's giving a free show."

"That's insufferable." She gave him a hard stare that would have melted a lesser man. "You are extremely rude. A gentleman would have made his presence known and would not have looked." She lifted her chin and turned away as if preparing to leave.

For some reason, he wasn't willing to let her go. Something about her intrigued him. "I meant no offense." He set down his rod and tackle box and held out his hands, palms up, to show he was harmless.

She didn't look like she was buying it. "Well, what you did was flat-out rude and insufferable. You're a perverted old white man."

"And you are a beautiful young black woman," he returned with a smile. "What are you doing out here?"

She glared at him. "Now you want me to carry on a conversation with you?"

"I came to fish, but don't let me bother you. There's plenty of room for both of us." Mathew picked up his gear and moved a safe distance away in the rough grass at the edge of the lake. "I realize you have finished swimming, but you're welcome to stay and relax. It's such a beautiful day; it would be a shame not to enjoy it."

He could use the company and what the hell, talking to her would be better than nothing, despite his beliefs. Besides, she was strikingly beautiful.

He watched her cautiously sit down on the bank, farther away than he would have liked. "What's your name?" he asked.

She eyed him warily, as if deciding how much to tell him. "Hannah. What's yours?"

"Mathew Stephens," he replied, casting his line into the lake. "So what is it you do? You must be one of those pretty house nannies." Even as the words left his mouth, he saw her expression tighten with anger.

"Excuse *me*," Hannah replied, her cheeks darkening. "A house nanny? I don't think so."

"Then what?" he said, baiting her further. He enjoyed watching her temper flare. "Are you a school teacher?"

"No," she answered, sitting up straight with a frown. "I'm an attorney."

"Really? That is surprising," he said, needling her further.

"What are you, some white trash farmer?" she said indignantly.

"Now look who's being rude," Mathew countered with a laugh. "I'm a judge."

Hannah looked him over from head to toe. "You sure don't look like a judge."

He stopped smiling, uncertain what she meant. "How is a judge supposed to look?"

"I'm not trying to insult you," she said with a dazzling smile. "It's a compliment. Many of the judges I know are old and fat, that's all."

Mathew smiled, surprised by his appreciation of her words. "Thank you. You're very attractive yourself."

Hannah looked away, gazing into the water as they shared a companionable silence for a while. Mathew realized he was flirting with a black woman, something totally alien to him as it went against everything he stood for, but she was so damned beautiful, he couldn't help himself. Watching her made his stomach tighten and his body yearn to feel the warmth of her skin and the heated passion of her kisses. What the hell was wrong with him?

Hannah looked up again, her face calm. "It would seem that you don't know much about fishing," she said.

"What do you mean?" He felt as though he had been caught staring, and it made him stammer. "I've been fishing all my life."

"It's a wonder you ever caught anything." Hannah got up and walked over to him until she was close enough to touch. She smelled of strawberries and lake water. "You *have* caught a fish before, haven't you?"

She took the fishing pole from him, reeled in the line, and cast it out into the water again. He studied her from the corner of his eye, painfully aware of her generous bosom and the way the damp shirt still clung to her body in the most fascinating way. He could see the outline of her nipples beneath the fabric, and found it difficult to think of anything else as a powerful wave of desire shot through his loins.

"I think I caught something," she cried, excitedly tugging on the line.

Unaware of the effect she was having on him, she struggled to reel it in. He stepped up behind her, and as he reached around to help her drag the large squirming fish onto the bank, his arms pressed against the warmth of her breasts. She felt good in his arms, firm and sweet smelling.

As soon as the fish lay gasping on the grass, he moved away before she could feel his arousal. She had landed a fat grayish black catfish with long whiskers.

"Nice catch," he said, watching her lean over to pull the hook expertly from its mouth. She obviously was a woman who didn't mind getting her hands dirty, and knew something about fishing; what an interesting combination.

"Your wife will be mighty happy when you bring that home," she said with a smile, holding up her wriggling catch.

Mathew's said nothing, his expression blank.

She looked up at him, the smile fading. "You're married with kids and stuff, right?"

"I'm a bachelor, never married," Mathew replied, watching her expression light up with amusement.

"I can't imagine why," Hannah replied, tilting her chin down to flash him a flirtatious look from beneath long lashes. "I'll tell you what. What would say to my cooking up a nice catfish dinner for us this evening?"

Taken aback by her directness, Mathew didn't know how to respond, and the question hung in the air between them until she began to look uncomfortable.

"I'm sorry," she said, her smile gone. "You probably have plans."

"No," Mathew replied, hesitantly. "Dinner would be... nice." He couldn't believe he had just accepted her invitation, but somehow, it seemed like the right thing to do.

"All right, then. I'll see you at six," she said, her smile back in full force. "Where do you live?"

Mathew found his head turning of its own accord toward his house. She followed his gaze.

"Is that your house up there?"

"My property ends at the other side of this lake," he replied. "And yes, that's my house."

"Good. I'll see you later, Mathew."

Mathew nodded, watching her walk away, the fish swinging from her right hand in time to the gentle sway of her hips. Without turning, she raised a hand in farewell.

He called out without thinking, "Don't be late."

Having decided not to go back to the office, she drove home. Hannah strolled into the kitchen, carrying what would soon be the main course for her and Mathew's dinner. Humming softly to herself, she placed the catfish in the sink and ran cold water over it. Her bad mood had evaporated almost as quickly as the water droplets on her skin.

Deborah Collins came into the kitchen, her dark brow knotted in a frown. Hannah knew her mother worried about her, and she probably should have checked in before she took off for the lake, but she had totally forgotten.

"What're you doing with that fish?" her mother asked curiously.

"I was at the lake down the road and saw this guy fishing the wrong way, so I showed him the right way to do it." She lifted the fish's head above the edge of the sink for her mother to see. "And I caught one."

The fish seemed to escape her mother's attention. Instead, she focused on the rest of the story. "What man?"

Hannah rolled her eyes. "Just a man, Ma. Would you do me a huge favor and clean and filet this for me? Please?"

Her mother looked the fish over with an expression of distaste. "For what?"

Hannah grabbed a dish towel and dried her hands. "Well, I promised to cook dinner for him."

"You what?" her mother asked as she raised her eyebrows. "Girl, what were you thinking?"

Hannah sighed. "It seemed the right thing to do. After all, it was his lake."

Deborah heard the defensiveness Hannah couldn't keep out of her voice and said, "All right," but Hannah could tell she wasn't happy about it.

She gave her mother a quick peck on the cheek. "I'm going to take a bath and get ready."

Her mother nodded as she quickly cleaned Hannah's catch.

As she started out of the kitchen, Hannah paused. "By the way, what did Geoff want with Daddy this morning?"

"He came by to warn us about the Klan," her mother said over her shoulder, throwing her daughter a worried look. "They have been pretty active lately, and he said they have their eyes on your Daddy."

"What would they want with Daddy?" Hannah frowned, walking back toward her mother.

Deborah Collins drew in a deep breath. "I don't know, but I want you to be extra careful about where you go and who you talk to. You hear me? That includes this man you're cooking dinner for."

"I promise, Ma." Hannah gave her mother a reassuring hug.

Deborah leaned against her daughter for a moment, then snatched the catfish from the sink and went back to her task, adding, "Crazy things have been happening in the community these days, and I don't want my family to become part of it."

Hannah went over to the kitchen table and sat, her bath forgotten for the moment. "I know, Ma. It'll be okay. You'll see."

"So who is this gentleman you're seeing tonight?" Mrs. Collins rinsed the scales off her hands, and opened a drawer to pull out a filet knife. With sure strokes, she slit the fish and removed its innards, and then neatly separated the bone from the soft flesh.

"I'm pretty sure you don't know him," Hannah answered, grabbing a crisp red apple from the bowl in the middle of the table and taking a bite. "His name is Mathew."

"Is he fine?" her mother asked with a sly smile.

"He's very handsome," Hannah said, remembering how he had made her feel. "He sounds lonely, though."

Her mother turned from the sink, her dark brows lowered. "What about Kenneth?"

Hannah sighed. "I saw him today at the lounge. He's still there playing his guitar and singing."

Her mother's frown deepened. "He's a nice boy... and handsome, too."

"But I don't feel anything for him." Hannah shrugged, wishing she could. Her parents obviously liked him. What she really wanted was love, a love that would last through the ages.

"Well, that happens sometimes," her mother agreed. "It was that way at first with your father and me."

"I know, Ma, but I want... I need more than that." She got up, and looked at her mother with regret. "I know it worked out for you and Daddy, but you were lucky. I don't want to start a marriage without love and hope that someday it will grow. I want to be swept off my feet, hopelessly and madly in love."

"I know, baby," her mother replied softly. "You run along now and take your bath while I finish up."

Hannah hastened upstairs to get ready. The thought of seeing Mathew again made her tingle as she drew water into the tub and added a generous portion of strawberry bubble bath. She couldn't understand why he had never married, or why some hungry white woman hadn't snapped him up long ago. He was charming and handsome, had money, and a big house, and she had found him quite funny, once she got over the shock of him seeing her naked. She blushed again, dropping her clothes on the bathroom floor and slipping into the soothing warmth of the scented bath.

The thought of him watching her as she frolicked in the lake did delicious things to her body. Had he been aroused when she emerged, water streaming down her creamy brown skin? Would he think about her firm hips and gently curved hips when she saw him tonight? And if he did, would his bedroom blue eyes darken with passion? Goosebumps swarmed up her arms at the thought, sending a sharp wave of desire through her.

It wasn't until she had toweled off and stood before her closet in a sheer camisole and matching panties that she remembered her mother's remarks about the Klan. How could someone be so brutal against another person's life and livelihood? How could it happen to them? Her father held the respect of the entire community, and his bakery served both black and white customers alike. Thank God for Geoff and his offer of help from the police force. Since they knew about the threat, the police would make sure her family remained safe, she convinced herself.

Finally settling on a peach flowered sundress and white sandals, she dressed, put on light make-up, and curled her reluctant hair into ringlets gathered at the back of her head. A quick spritz of Lily-of-the-Valley perfume, and she was ready to go. She twirled once in front of the full-length mirror, mounted on her bathroom door, and went downstairs.

She glanced at the clock; five-forty. "I'm going, Ma. Thanks for helping out."

Grabbing her purse and the bag with the fish from the fridge, Hannah trotted out the door.

Chapter Eight

Mathew's doorbell rang at quarter of six.

"You're early," he commented when he opened the door. He hadn't been sure she would show up, and now that she was here, he wasn't certain what he should do.

"I'm here," Hannah replied. "That's the main thing."

As she walked past him, he closed the door, admiring the way her hips swayed when she moved.

"Here's the fish," she said, holding up a large Ziploc bag. "How about showing me the way to the kitchen?"

He led her down a long hallway, passing the living room, formal dining room, half bath, study, and finally through the last door, which led into a large kitchen filled with every modern convenience a cook could desire. The appliances were brushed stainless steel and appeared to have been purchased during the past five years. Hardwood floors and cupboards were made from solid cherry, forest wood granite topped the counters, and the walls had been painted a creamy ivory.

"Nice kitchen," Hannah said, but inwardly she thought, *I hate stainless steel!*

"Thanks," Mathew said. "Although I can't take all the credit; my interior designer picked out the major appliances."

It figures.

Moving to the island in the center of the large room, Mathew sat on a bar stool, also made of cherry, and watched as she pulled down a cast iron skillet from the overhead rack. He admired the delicate curve of her neck and the way her flowered dress molded to every nuance of her body.

"Are you just going to stare at me all evening?" she joked, giving him a flirtatious glance over her shoulder.

"I wasn't sure you would come," he said. But he had given the help the night off, just in case.

"Why?" she replied, looking back at him with large brown eyes. When he didn't answer, she smiled with satisfaction and pulled open the doors of the double refrigerator, peering inside before pulling out a pound of Colby cheese. From the pantry, she gathered a box of pasta and a can of sweet potatoes.

"So what are we having?" he asked, enjoying the ease with which she made herself at home in his spotless kitchen. "I amazed you can find anything."

"I can find my way around a kitchen."

An hour later, Hannah plated the food and joined Mathew in the living room where he sat watching the news.

"Dinner is ready, master," Hannah said with a curtsey, trying to look subservient and failing miserably.

Mathew jumped up out of his chair, his face red. "You don't have to call me, master."

He looked so anxious she couldn't help giggling. "I was joking. Geez, where's your sense of humor?"

Mathew looked relieved, and smiled, following Hannah into the dining room where dinner waited. She had gone to a lot of extra trouble, setting the table with attractive precision, complemented by artistically arranged food. The gleaming cherry wood table reflected the flames as she lit two burgundy tapers she had found in the china cabinet against one wall, giving the room a cozy, romantic glow.

"What do you think?" Hannah asked. "We have fried fish, macaroni and cheese, and sweet potatoes. I even brought along a good bottle of wine."

He picked up the wine and examined the label. "I didn't see that when you came in."

"That is one of the reasons why women like big purses," she explained with a satisfied smile.

Mathew held her chair for her, and then took his place at the head of the table. He swept the white linen napkin onto his lap and lifted a forkful of fish.

"This food is amazing," Mathew complimented her after a few silent mouthfuls.

"Thank you," she replied, reaching for her wine glass to allow him fill it. "Either you are really sweet, or you're not used to eating a home-cooked meal."

"I just appreciate good food," Mathew shot her a look, "and good company."

She felt her cheeks warming, and hurried to change the subject. "So what do you do besides judge and hand out sentences?"

"A lot of things," he said between mouthfuls of food. "I work on my land and fish."

She looked him over, admiring the firm length of his body. He looked fit and healthy. "Is that all?"

"That's the main stuff," he said, his smile disappearing, as if he wanted to discourage her from taking that line of conversation any further.

"That can't be all you do." Hannah sipped her wine, watching his face. His expression seemed almost troubled.

"Occasionally I go out with friends." Mathew quickly changed the course of the conversation. "How about you?"

"I like to read," she replied, her eyes downcast. The boys she went to school with had considered her intellect an unattractive quality, but so far, Mathew did not seem to mind. "And I love to swim and travel. I do a lot of things."

Hannah glanced up from her plate to find him staring at her with an appraising glint in his blue eyes.

"I'm sure a pretty girl like you has men fawning all over her," Mathew said.

"Maybe, but I'm hardly ever interested. I usually attract the wannabes or the scrubs who like to hang out at home with their mamas." Hannah laughed. "What about you? I still can't believe you're single."

"I'm usually too busy for romance," he shrugged, finishing the last of his food. He leaned back and patted his stomach.

She frowned at him with mock annoyance. "A man should never be too busy for love." She picked up her wine glass and raised it to her lips, letting the cool white wine slide down her throat.

"I have some vanilla ice cream in the freezer," he said, sitting forward with a mischievous grin. "Would you like to enjoy some on my back patio?"

"Sure." Hannah smiled.

They cleared the table, working together as if they had been partners for years.

A huge pecan tree shaded the patio, and the rocking chairs creaked against the wood flooring as they ate their ice cream, hers plain, his with a dribble of chocolate syrup on top. Twilight crept up from the corners of the big yard and held them in its warm embrace, with no light or noise to disrupt the perfect silence.

"Hannah, you look beautiful tonight." Mathew's words vibrated between them, as though he had left a lot more unsaid.

She kept staring out at the horizon, but his words held her captive. For the first time in a long time, she didn't know what to say, so she didn't say anything.

"Earlier you said you were an attorney," he said after a moment. "Where do you work? I don't recall ever seeing you around the courthouse."

"I work in Jackson," she said, thankful that the awkward moment had passed.

"I'm surprised you wanted to be an attorney," he joked. "I didn't think that would be something a woman like you would be interested in."

"And why not?" she asked with an edge to her voice, wishing she could see him better in the twilight. "What would a woman like me be interested in? Making babies, cooking dinner for some white family?" She couldn't keep the anger from creeping into her voice. If she hadn't known better, she would think he was prejudiced.

"I meant no offense. I'm surprised that's all. I just never figured you for a lawyer; I thought you were joking when you told me that earlier." Mathew's voice held apology, and something else she couldn't identify.

"What court do you work for?" Hannah asked, stirring her ice cream into a slow puddle of liquid. She had lost the taste for it now.

"I work here in Crystal Springs," he said, and she could almost see him puffing up his chest. He sounded proud of his position on the bench, but to Hannah, it sounded more like he was tooting his own horn.

"It's strange I never heard of you before." She searched her memory for any mention of a Judge Stephens, but nothing came to mind.

"I sometimes get cases transferred from Jackson," he replied. "I just got one concerning a man who was being sued by his ex-wife."

"Oh, my God," Hannah said. "I passed on that one. Jason Tibbs." It was less a question than a statement; she knew the case well. Tibbs had rubbed her the wrong way, but she had done her best to get him the right judicial setting.

"That's him." Mathew laughed. "I have to admit, you sound like a smart woman."

Hannah heard the sincerity in his voice. "Thank you," she answered, feeling her cheeks grow hot again. The energy between them made her excited and vulnerable at the same time, and she wasn't sure she liked either feeling. Listening to the crickets sing, she said, "I should be going. It's getting late."

"Yes, it is," Mathew replied.

As Hannah got up to take her bowl to the kitchen, her foot caught on the leg of the swing and she fell forward, right into Mathew's lap. The bowls clattered, forgotten, to the porch while the two of them stared intensely into each other's eyes for several long moments. Then Mathew moved in and kissed her, his lips burning against hers as her arms slid around his neck. Seconds later, Hannah pulled away and rose shakily to her feet, relieved that he couldn't see the color flaring more deeply in her cheeks. How could she have done that? How could he? They barely knew each other.

As if he read her thoughts, Mathew distracted her by saying, "Don't worry about the bowls. I'll see you out."

She allowed him take her elbow and lead her through the house and out to the driveway.

He opened the door of her car. "Drive safely."

Hannah hesitated a moment before speaking. "I had a great time tonight, Mathew. Thank you." She got in, and he closed the door.

"Me, too," he whispered.

When she started her car to drive away, Mathew turned away and headed for the house, but stopped, turned, and called out to her. Hannah lowered her window as he hurried back to her car.

He looked almost boyish in the fading light, his hair ruffled and a youthful grin on his handsome face. "Hannah, you're welcome to come back any time."

She smiled at him, suddenly shy. "I might just take you up on that offer."

He watched her drive away, and then turned to go inside the house, acutely aware of how big and silent it suddenly felt. In the kitchen, he rinsed the bowls he had retrieved from the patio, placed them in the dishwasher, and tidied up so his cook wouldn't find a mess. Then he climbed the stairs to get ready for bed. His lips still tingled from the kiss he had shared with Hannah, her soft lips melding with his warm ones, her firm breasts pressed close against him. Just thinking about it made his body ache for her.

He couldn't deny it. He wanted her.

On top of that thought came another, more chilling one. He wanted a black woman, a woman the color whose race he had chosen to hate and to kill, if necessary, to reclaim the supreme right of the white man's rule in this country. And even though he knew it went against everything he had ever thought, believed, or learned, he still wanted her.

This can't be happening, he thought, leaning against the cold porcelain steel sink as he tried to brush his teeth. Could this be temptation from the Devil? He shook his head, glaring at the pale face in the mirror, trying to pull himself together.

Come on, Mathew, you need to overcome this.

Later, as he lay between the cool cotton sheets of his oversized bed, he turned off the bedside lamp, and thought again about how beautiful she was, her skin the creamy smoothness of café au lait and her hair the color of dark, forbidden chocolate. How would she feel here next to him? He desperately wanted to find out.

He had seen women of almost every race, but something about Hannah truly captured his heart. Mathew admired her energy and her beautiful smile, so contagious it made his heart feel light as a feather. He also liked the way she looked at him, as a man, without color or prejudice. She was everything he desired in a woman, except she was black.

He glanced at the nightstand and a picture of himself sitting alongside his fellow Klansmen. Although he couldn't make out the details in the darkness of the room, he knew the picture from memory – could see the group of men with big smiles of camaraderie on their faces. They had shared a lot of good times, a lot of beliefs, a lot of hatred. They would not allow him to falter. He could rely on that, but somehow, that thought brought no comfort. Mathew turned his head and stared at the textured ceiling.

"Regardless of all the reasons I shouldn't, I really want to see Hannah Collins again," he whispered to the darkness.

* * *

Danny Pummel was up early the following morning and, almost without thinking, he grabbed the throwaway cell and dialed Geoff's number.

As soon as Geoff picked up, he said, "G, I'm going over my notes from Sunday. Did I mention Ken Lewis was at the meeting?"

"I guess we were so overwhelmed by the other members that we overlooked the small fish. No, you didn't mention him," Geoff said.

"Well, he was there." Danny knew that Geoff was still worried about him joining the Klan, so he kept talking, hoping to ease the strain in his friend's voice. "I'll see what else I can find out at the next meeting."

Gray Love

"At least that confirms that the station wagon Mrs. Henderson described belongs to him," Geoff growled. "That lying bastard."

"I'll call you after the meeting next Sunday if I find out anything new," Danny said.

"Right," Geoff replied impatiently.

"Did you warn Mr. Collins and his family?"

"Yes," Geoff replied. "I did that yesterday morning."

"Okay, here's what I need you to do. I want you to bring Ken Lewis in for questioning," Danny instructed. "Then call Mrs. Henderson, and find out if she is willing to identify his vehicle."

"That's what the Chief suggested. I'm on it."

"Okay," Danny said. "Talk to you soon."

After Geoff disconnected, he hurried out to his car and headed to the station to tell Chief Waldron his plans.

After a brief knock, he entered his boss's office. "Chief, I heard from Danny this morning, and there are a couple of things we need to do."

Waldron put down his newspaper. "What's going on?"

"Danny said that Ken Lewis was at the meeting, too," Geoff said in a rush. "That means his station wagon probably was the one Mrs. Henderson saw at her house."

His expression hopeful, the older man nodded. "I'll get a couple officers to bring him in, while you go pick up Mrs. Henderson and take her to see Lewis's vehicle."

An hour later, Geoff knocked loudly on Mrs. Henderson's door, hoping she was home.

She opened the door slowly, looking ten years older than she had the week before. "Hello, Lieutenant. Is everything okay?"

Geoff nodded. "I would like you to come with me to see if you can identify one of the vehicles from the night your husband was murdered."

Jill returned his gaze, her face lined with worry. She looked like she hadn't slept in days, and he could tell she had lost weight by the looseness of her jeans.

"I don't want any more trouble for me and my family, Lieutenant."

"Jill," he said quietly, trying to soothe her fears, "you don't have to see anyone, just a car. The owner is downtown being questioned so he won't know you went there." Her expression didn't change, so he added, "You would be helping to get these people off the streets. It's important that you do this before the Klan targets another family."

She gazed at him for several long seconds. Sighing, her shoulders drooped. "Okay, fine. Just let me put on my shoes."

On their way to the auto shop, she cried softly, and he glanced over to see her crumpled against the passenger side window.

"Are you all right?" Geoff gently asked.

She sniffed and took a deep breath before answering. "No, I'm not. I don't think I will ever be all right again. I wish those Klan people were all dead."

"Now, Jill, you can't go around hating white folks because of a few bad apples." Even as he said the words, Geoff wasn't sure he completely believed it himself. But he knew he had to try to give her back some of the peace she had lost the day her husband was brutally murdered. He truly believed there was hope for everyone, if they could only get past the hate.

"There are a select few, just like certain blacks who join their own hate organizations. None of it makes any sense," he said. "Naturally, we should all be proud of who we are, but we need to mingle with different cultures to learn the beauty of this world. Each race has so much to offer."

She sighed. "I guess you're right. I know better. I have some wonderful, caring white friends who are just as outraged about this as we are. Let's just bring the men who murdered my Taylor to justice."

"Now you're talking," Geoff smiled.

A moment later, he stopped the car in front of the garage. "We're here. Does that car look familiar?" Geoff pointed to the station wagon, still sitting in the same spot.

She started crying again, trembling in her seat. "Oh Lord Jesus, I can't believe this. He's not here, is he?"

"I told you he wasn't. Now don't worry about that," he assured her. "We hauled him in for questioning. Is that the station wagon you saw that night?"

She got out of the car and walked slowly toward the vehicle, her tennis shoes scuffing up whirls of dirt from the dry ground. Running her hand along the dark blue body of the dusty car, she stopped when she reached the rear tailgate.

"What is it, Jill?"

"This is it." Her voice was filled with anger, and beneath the anger, pain and conviction.

He laid a hand on her thin shoulder. "Are you certain?"

"When the men drove off, the station wagon went first. The headlights from the other cars lit up a shiny pirate sticker on the right side." She pointed at the car. "That same sticker right there and there was mud on the bumper and covering the license plate. This car has mud spots and the license plate is still covered."

She started shivering, and Geoff took off his uniform jacket and draped it across her shoulders.

She looked up at him, her paleness sharply defining the dark circles beneath her soulful brown eyes. "I hope I did everything right. I can't take any more of this."

"You did just fine," he said, his arm around her shoulders. She hid her face against him for a moment. "Come on, I'll take you home now."

She said nothing all the way back to her house. As she got out of the car, she turned to him, a worried expression on her haggard face.

"That man isn't going to come after me, is he? Me and my family are safe, right?"

Geoff nodded. "Right, you have nothing to worry about."

She lifted her chin and slowly walked to her front door. Before going inside, she turned and waved.

When Geoff arrived back at the station, Chief Waldron was in the interrogation room with Ken Lewis. Geoff opened the door and motioned for the Chief to step out.

"What did you find out?" he asked Geoff as soon as he had closed the door behind him.

Geoff glanced through the one-way window. Ken Lewis looked nervous. Good.

"Mrs. Henderson identified the vehicle as being the station wagon that was there that night."

"Was she positive?" Waldron asked, his voice sounding urgent. Geoff knew the Chief wanted to get these guys almost as bad as he did. The KKK had been a stain on Waldron's spotless record for far too long.

Geoff explained about the mud and the pirate sticker.

"Well, that's good enough to hold him," the Chief said, scratching his head. "I'm going to keep him here until we get some answers."

As they were about to walk into the interrogation room, Danny arrived and joined them. When he approached the window, he saw Ken Lewis sitting inside, staring at the two-way mirror and wondering what kind of evidence they had against him.

"Danny," Geoff greeted him. "We've got Lewis."

"What's going on?" Danny asked, his gaze going to the man sitting alone in the interrogation room.

"We're putting his ass in jail," the Chief said with a satisfied smile.

"What?" Danny exclaimed, his eyebrows rising. "You can't do that. He'll think I set the Klan up."

"I'm sorry you have to disappoint your new friends," the Chief said sarcastically.

"You don't understand, Chief. This will ruin everything. We won't be able to stop the rest of them, if I don't find out more about the next attack," Danny said, shaking his head. "We have to catch them in the act."

The Chief looked at him, but remained silent. Geoff didn't know what to say, either, so he said nothing, letting Danny convince his boss this was the right thing to do.

"Let me walk in there with Geoff and release him, so he'll think I'm on their side," Danny pleaded.

"Danny, I'm sorry, but no," Waldron said firmly. "We know he helped murder Taylor Henderson. He's staying put." When Danny continued to look worried, the Chief laid a hand on his shoulder. "Look, he's not going to blame you. We have an eyewitness that identified his car as being on the scene that night."

"Who?"

"Jill Henderson, but don't worry, I'm not telling him who the witness is."

Danny looked at Geoff. "Expect my call."

As he turned to walk out, Geoff followed him. "I'll walk you to the door."

They made their way to the cool, tiled lobby. Geoff led his friend past the ancient water cooler to stand near the iron-barred door, away from the front desk and any foot traffic coming through.

"Take it easy, Danny," he said. "The Chief is right. Lewis will be told that we're holding him because of the vehicle. I questioned him twice about both the Klan and his vehicle. He'll never suspect you. I've been in his face too much for that."

"I know, G, I'm just on edge."

"Look, it will all be over soon, and your work will have made a difference. If it weren't for you, we would still be chasing down bad leads."

Danny grinned at Geoff. "True enough," he said.

"When do you think the raid will happen?" Geoff asked.

"The Judge said something about Wednesday of next week. I'll find out for sure at the next meeting," Danny replied.

"Call and give me the time, okay?"

"You got it," Danny agreed.

"I have to admit, Danny, you have guts," Geoff said.

The other man nodded. "Yeah, and stupidity, as my wife often tells me."

Geoff slapped his back. "But just think of the lives you'll be saving."

Danny's expression hardened. "Yes, there is that. I just wish that people wouldn't hate each other enough to kill, just because they look a little different."

"Amen to that," Geoff said, smiling sadly. "Amen to that."

Chapter Nine

Hannah sat in McCafferty's Café with two of her best friends. Melody Huntley, a district attorney in Jackson, had red hair, green eyes, and a fiery disposition when it came to going after the bad guys. Ava Clutcheon was a raven-haired beauty with a coffee and cream complexion, who was a homemaker with a husband and three children. Both had been Hannah's friends since elementary school. While waiting for their food, they chatted about clothes, movies, and life in general. Hannah sipped from her glass of water, and when the food came, in the sudden stillness at the table, she asked, "Have either of you heard of a man named Mathew Stephens?"

"I have," Melody replied, unfolding her napkin and dropping into her lap. "Why do you ask?" Melody's beautiful green eyes held a warning.

Hannah asked anyway, "What do you know about him?"

"I know to stay far away from him," Melody said, her voice hard. "He's a judge, and he pretty well does whatever he wants with anything and anybody."

"What makes you say that?" Hannah wondered why her friend sounded so upset with Mathew, so she pressed on.

"He's a man, isn't he? And," Melody added conspiratorially, "I hear he is with the Klan."

"What!" Hannah and Ava exclaimed together. Hannah's fork dropped to her plate, her food forgotten. "No."

Her friend nodded. "Some folks say he's the Grand Wizard." Her voice had steadily dropped to a whisper.

"That can't be true," Hannah interrupted. "The Klan killed Mr. Henderson just last week. A judge doesn't kill; he metes out justice."

"Exactly," Melody went on. "And that's exactly what the KKK calls it."

Ava glanced around warily. "Let's talk about something else. Have you read the latest Nora Roberts book yet?"

And the conversation went on, past the darkness of the Ku Klux Klan, and on to more ordinary things like shoes, books, and babies. Hannah let the conversation flow around her, nodding or laughing when appropriate, but her food remained untouched on her plate as her mind raced, refusing to ignore the implications of Mathews possible connection to the KKK. How could he be part of something so evil? She pushed her salad around, remembering their dinner together, the passionate kiss, and his smile as she left. He wouldn't have touched, kissed, or even become friends with her if he belonged to the KKK, especially if he was the Grand Wizard. The fact that he was white and she was black meant nothing to her. He hadn't shown the slightest distaste for her food or her company. Hannah remembered her teasing referral to him as master, and his surprise when she said it. It just wasn't possible that he was a Klan member, much less their leader.

She examined her two friends, one white and one black. Their color had never made a difference in how they felt about each other. How could Mathew see them differently because of their skin color? Hannah shook her head, glad her friends had changed the subject instead of pursuing why she had brought up his name in the first place. Maybe she had seen a side of him that others hadn't. Ava and Melody would never believe her if she told them about her dinner with Mathew, so she remained silent, limiting her responses to occasional comments about their ongoing conversation. Her mind whirled as she thought about Mathew and his possible involvement with the Klan.

Back at her office after the interminable lunch, Hannah finished her cases for the day, still thinking about Mathew. She decided to look up the Ku Klux Klan on the Internet and found a link for the Klan's official website. Out of curiosity, she clicked on the link and began reading articles about white supremacy.

Her heart tightened with every word, every act of hate, and the violence that was promoted on the screen. Pictures of white men in white masks, afraid to show their cowardly faces to the rest of the world, made her stomach clench and nausea rise to her throat. Hannah's world swung in the balance, her feelings for Mathew struggling against the immoral blackness portrayed by the society with which he supposedly belonged. Somehow, she had to discover the truth.

As Hannah drove home, she couldn't stop thinking about the things she had learned today. She could not deny the attraction she felt for the stranger by the lake, and knew it would be so easy to fall in love with him. And yet, the images from the computer haunted her, making her wonder she would ever learn the truth, even as she tried to convince herself that Melody's statements had been nothing more than idle gossip… but what if her friend's suspicions were true?

When she arrived home, her mother greeted her at the kitchen door. "Hello, dear, how was your day?"

"What's wrong?" Hannah's stomach knotted. Had something happened to her father? "You usually don't meet me at the door."

"Nothing is wrong, honey. I was washing a few dishes and saw you pull up," her mother reassured her. "You look so tired; it worries me."

Hannah managed a brief smile. "I *am* tired. I think I'll go upstairs, take a nice hot bath, and lie down before dinner."

Deborah took her daughter's briefcase and suit jacket out of her hands and shooed her toward the steps. "You do that."

Upstairs, Hannah pulled her blouse out of her skirt and began to unbutton it. As soon as she turned on the water, the phone rang.

"I'll get it," Hannah shouted, running over to pick up the extension in her room. She dropped her blouse on the bed and answered. "Hello?"

"Hi, Hannah," the man's voice made her heart lift for a moment, until he said, "Its Kenneth."

Hannah sighed, slipping out of her skirt. "Hi, Ken. What's up?"

"I was just thinking about you," he said softly. "I can't wait till Friday. I want to take you to that new Italian restaurant over on Fourth Street."

"What?" She kept her eye on the tub, only half paying attention. "Oh, Angelino's? That sounds nice. What time are you coming?"

"Be ready at seven-thirty, baby," Kenneth said. "I can't wait to see you again."

"I'll be ready," she replied distractedly. "Bye, Kenneth."

She hung up the phone and hurried into the bathroom to turn off the water, mixing in a handful of bath salts that filled the air with the scent of spring flowers. Stepping into the tub, she lowered herself into the steamy water, letting the silky warmth soothe her senses and float her away to Mathew's back porch and the scorching kiss they had shared. Hannah moved restlessly, wanting more, her hands delicately touching the soft skin of her breasts, circling her aching nipples before sliding down to her flat stomach and over her tender inner thighs.

Mathew's hands would feel like this, a gentle touch probing the secret recesses of her body.

"Oh, I would love to kiss him again," she murmured, her fingers slipping lower and deeper, stirring her arousal until all she could think about was what it would feel like to receive his velvety hardness bringing passionate cries of satisfaction to her swollen lips. Long after the water cooled, she lay there satisfied, dreaming of Mathew's touch.

She climbed out of the tub, and toweled herself off with a large fluffy pink towel before smoothing lavender-scented lotion along her tingling skin. Every time she touched herself, she imagined what his hands would feel like, and her skin glowed at the thought of his hands stroking her in places no man had ever touched. Until now, she had never met a man who stirred her passions the way he did.

Hannah dressed and went downstairs to help her mother prepare dinner. Her father was already seated at the table, his newspaper spread out before him and a cold glass of lemonade next to his hand.

She leaned over to give his stumbled cheek a kiss. "Hi, Daddy."

Her father smiled up at her, folding his paper and putting it aside. "Hi, sugar. You sure look fine this evening."

Hannah blushed, looking down at the blue scooped-neck T-shirt and paisley skirt she had chosen. "These old things?" she countered lightly, sitting across from him.

"Very fetching," he said with a wink. "You look like you have a date."

"No date, Daddy. I just wanted to look nice for you." She smiled and glanced over at her mother, hoping her father would drop this line of questioning. "Can I help you with anything, Ma?"

Her mother shook her head. "No, darling, not tonight; why don't you pour yourself a glass of lemonade and relax."

"Your Mama says you fancy some man."

Obviously, he didn't want to give it up. Hannah searched for something to say, but ended up answering, "Oh, Daddy, you know how Ma always makes a big deal out of everything."

Her mother snorted inelegantly. "Girl, you know what I'm talking about," she said. "Stop trying to deny it. I've never seen you act the way you have since you met that man."

Even as Hannah shook her head, her father asked, "Well, are we going to meet him? What's he like?"

"He's just a nice, attractive man with a good job," Hannah said. "I'm not a teenager, you know. I'm thirty-six, for heaven's sake."

"Something must be going on," her father replied. "You're mama told me that you cooked dinner for him, and you're walking around glowing like you have just won the lottery."

Hannah's cheeks grew warm again, but she kept her expression neutral. "Well, I *am* thinking about seeing him again tomorrow."

"Go see him then, and maybe someday you will have a family of your own," her father joked.

"Sure, Daddy, whatever," she said with a grin, and got up to help her mother carry the food to the table. For some reason, she was hungry now, and piled her plate high with roast beef, mashed potatoes, and steamed asparagus.

Just as she raised a forkful of meat to her mouth, her mother suggested, "How about inviting your young gentleman over for dinner on Saturday?"

Hannah almost choked; glad she hadn't managed to get the food into her mouth. "I don't think that would be a good idea."

"Why not?" her mother asked. "Are you ashamed of him?"

"No," she answered, searching for the right thing to say. "He's just different from the other guys I've dated. Besides, we just met."

"What do you mean, different?"

"He's very... professional," Hannah finished lamely. With all this KKK business and her doubts about Mathew, bringing up the fact that he was white seemed less than appropriate, at least for now. Seeing her mother's disappointed look, she added, "I'll think about it, okay?"

Deborah examined her daughter's face. Whatever she saw there, she let it go, picking up her fork. "Okay. Now eat so you can get some meat on those bones, baby," Mrs. Collins replied.

Hannah smiled as she ate her dinner.

At eight o'clock, she sat on her bed, half-heartedly working on a couple case studies, but her thoughts kept drifting back to Mathew and the lunch she'd had with her friends. The entire conversation still bothered her, and the thought that Mathew, with his hot glances and burning lips, might be involved with the Klan made her heart tighten painfully.

After trying unsuccessfully to focus on the files in front of her, Hannah gave up, closing the folder with a sigh. She had to do something, and the only thing she could think of was to go over to Mathew's house and ask him about the accusations. Her mind made up, Hannah got up and splashed cool water on her face before changing into a pair of jeans and a tank top and heading over to Mathew's house.

Mathew's elegant Victorian crouched in the moonlight like a giant monster waiting to devour her. Hannah shivered as goose bumps covered her arms. Taking a deep breath, she climbed the porch steps and rang the doorbell. After several moments, she decided no one was home and turned to leave.

The door behind her opened with a sudden rush, and Mathew's voice followed her down the steps. "Hey, come back. I'm home."

She turned, looking up at him. "Hello, Mathew," she said, hoping he wouldn't hear the slight tremble in her voice.

He watched her come back up the steps, and opened the door wider. "So what brings you here so late? Is anything wrong?"

She shook her head, level with him now, and said, "I couldn't stop thinking about the night we had together." Even as the words left her mouth, Hannah felt heat race up her neck and into her cheeks. She was glad the darkness hid the betraying color.

"Come on in," he said, smiling.

She walked inside, looking around with more interest this time, as if his home would tell her the truth of the accusation that had been made against him. It was just a house. A very nice one that she loved to be in, with no telltale signs of hatred and violence.

Mathew showed Hannah into the living room, offering her a seat on a wine-colored brocade couch. He sat opposite her in a matching wingback chair, and his eyes searched her face. "Something is wrong, Hannah. Talk to me."

Hannah looked deep into Mathew's blue eyes, and the concern in them made her blurt out, "I heard that you are the Grand Wizard of the local KKK."

She watched as his eyes widen, and then he asked, "Where did you hear that garbage?"

Hannah couldn't tell from his reaction what was going on inside his head, so she pressed further. "Why would there be such a rumor, if it wasn't true?" she countered.

He almost didn't wait for her to finish. "This town is a rumor mill. People say a lot of things about each other, sometimes out of jealously, sometimes out of spite, but that doesn't make them true."

Hannah released the breath she hadn't realized she had been holding, scanning his face for some indication of how he felt, or if she had offended him by asking. The only indication of anything was a slight sheen of moisture across his upper lip. She nodded. "True. So what are you doing tonight?"

"Nothing," he said with a puzzled frown. "I was in my study, organizing some files. Why?"

"Let me help," Hannah offered, wanting to spend time with him. He hadn't answered her accusation. At least, he hadn't made an outright denial, but right now it no longer mattered. She wanted to be with him. And if he had a problem with racial boundaries, she hadn't seen any evidence of it yet. Besides, if he really hated blacks, he would be interested in her, would he? In fact, his previous kiss spoke of an entirely different reaction.

"No, thank you." He shook his head.

"I insist."

Mathew smiled. "Okay. I'll be right back."

He went to his office and returned to the living room a few minutes later with a huge stack of papers and file folders. He set them before her on the coffee table. "There you go."

Hannah looked down at the papers piled before her. "That's a lot of work."

"I wasn't kidding when I said I was busy," he said. "But if you want to help, put the papers highlighted in blue in the blue file, the papers highlighted in green into the green file, and so on."

"I think I can handle that," she said with a smile.

The two of them started on the files. Mathew glanced at Hannah periodically as they worked, and each time, she met his gaze with one of her own before turning back to the task at hand. The air between them seemed to throb with electricity, making Hannah want to push the papers to the floor and throw herself into his arms. Instead, she focused on the colors, matching each paper to the appropriate folder, trying to still her heated thoughts with mindless repetition.

Time seemed to stand still while they worked, energy sparking every time their hands inadvertently touched. Before long, they were finished, and sat staring at each other across the neatly organized files.

"I appreciate your help tonight," he said softly. "It made a tedious task much more enjoyable."

Hannah lowered her gaze, suddenly nervous, wondering if he would kiss her again and knowing that more than anything, she wanted to feel the heated touch of his lips against hers. "You're welcome."

He hesitated a moment, then said, "Would you like to join me on my boat tomorrow evening? I could pick you up from work."

"I can't. I'm in court all day," she said reluctantly.

"What time do you get out of court?"

"Eight o'clock," she replied.

"Then how about I pick you up in front of the Jackson Courthouse at eight-fifteen?"

Hannah found herself giving in. "Sure. Why not?"

She looked at her watch, surprised at how late it was. "Good Lord. It's after eleven, and I have to get up early tomorrow. I should be going."

Mathew nodded, rising to offer her a hand up from the couch. "Okay. Thanks for stopping by tonight."

Hannah walked with Mathew to the front door, and then turned to face him. "I'm so happy you're not in the KKK. You wouldn't lie to me, would you, Mathew?" She searched his face for the truth.

His face gave nothing away as he said, "Have you seen the woman I fancy?"

It was a strange way of reminding her that that he 'fancied' a woman of color. But he seemed sincere by the way he looked at her and allowed his fingers linger against her skin whenever he touched her.

She smiled. "I guess not," she said, wondering why once more he hadn't exactly answered question.

Kissing his cheek, she whispered, "See you tomorrow."

The next morning while he was getting ready for work, Mathew Stephens answered a call from Reverend Butler. "Hello, Mathew. I hate to bother you so early."

"That's okay," Mathew said, propping the phone between his cheek and shoulder while he tied his tie. "Is anything wrong?"

"Yes, I'm afraid there is," the Reverend said grimly. "Ken Lewis is in jail. They're holding him because of that Henderson murder."

"What?" Mathew almost dropped the phone. How the hell had they connected Ken to that shooting? And with that thought came another. How could he lie to Hannah about his connection with the Klan?

The Reverend's words faded in and out until Mathew returned his attention to what he was saying.

"Yes, he's locked up right now. We need to get him out. You know Kenneth. He's a weak link. No telling how they might threaten him, and if he thinks it will save his own hide, he will rat us out without a second thought."

"I knew this was going to be a problem. Damn it, Reverend, how did we allow these murders to happen? I wanted to scare those men... put them in their place, not kill them," Mathew said.

"The boys just got a little carried away, Mathew," the Reverend said. "You know how passionate they are about the cause."

"That's fine," Mathew replied, tightly clenching the phone receiver, "but I don't ever want it happening again. It brings too much heat down on us." He paused. "Look, let's leave Ken where he is for now, and try to find out what kind of evidence they have against him. We have to be careful how we handle this. I don't want to risk exposing to the rest of us. Then on Sunday night, we'll talk it over and see what our next move will be. Right now, I need to get to work."

"I understand," Reverend Butler responded. "I'll send Luke over to visit Ken today to remind him to keep his mouth shut and make sure he doesn't say anything incriminating."

"You do that. Take care until Sunday."

Mathew hung up, still thinking about Hannah.

"Am I so lonely that I long for any woman who happens to show a little interest in me?" he asked the mirror. His reflection gave him no answers. Mathew pictured her at the lake, her long hair floating on the water as she swam. He remembered their sensual kiss, the softness of her full lips, and the satin expanse of skin beneath his hands. Even as he thought of her, passion gripped him in a tight hold, and it was an effort to move toward the front door.

* * *

Hannah sat next to her mother, reading the morning newspaper and drinking coffee. "Is today going to be another hard day?" her mother asked, refilling Hannah's cup.

"I don't think so," Hannah replied, moving the paper aside. "It should be okay."

"Shall I expect you for dinner?" her mother persisted.

Hannah remembered Mathew's invitation and shook her head. "I'm working late, so don't bother. I'll get something to eat afterward."

"Do you have a date?" her mother asked with a knowing grin.

"Ma, I'll be with Mathew." She returned her mother's smile.

"You've been seeing him a lot, Hannah. I think you had better let us meet this man."

"We've known each other less than a week, Ma. I don't want to scare him off by insisting he meet my parents already. Give it some time, and I promise, I'll ask him, but I really have to get to work now."

Hannah gathered her briefcase and keys and walked out to her car. She couldn't wait until work was over so she could see Mathew again. She wondered if he felt the same way about her. The thought curled through her, leaving happiness in its wake. Tonight would be special for both of them; she would see to it.

* * *

At the police station, Luke Fields arrived to visit Ken Lewis. Geoff watched him from his desk near the back of the office.

"May I help you, sir?" the desk sergeant asked Luke.

"Yes, sir, I'm here to visit Ken Lewis."

"Your name?" The officer looked him over.

"Luke Fields."

"Please sign right here," the sergeant said, pointing to the clipboard he laid on the counter.

Luke signed the visitor's form and handed it back.

"Go straight down that hall and to the left," he pointed in the right direction, "and tell the officers who you're here to see. They'll handle it from there."

Geoff watched Luke make his way toward the indicated hallway, passing the Chief's office along the way. The Chief glanced up at Luke, and then over to Geoff with a foreboding expression. Geoff nodded and followed the visitor as unobtrusively as possible. Maybe he could overhear them talking and find out something from the visit.

Two jailers met Luke in the hallway.

"Can I help you?" one of them asked.

Luke stopped in front of them. "I'm here to see Ken Lewis."

"Are you his attorney?"

"No, just a friend."

"Don't know as I would admit to being a friend of the Klan," the officer snickered, elbowing his buddy. "That's what they call him here in the jail. I reckon he ain't too popular with the other prisoners."

"That's nice, officers," Luke said slowly. Geoff saw the man's hands clench, but his voice remained even. "You shouldn't accuse a man of being something he isn't."

The larger of the two guards, George Graham, looked like a linebacker for Mississippi State. He scratched his nearly bald head, looking down at Ken. "I don't get you people. I'm white and proud of it, but I don't hate others because of their color. God is the only one who should judge."

Geoff saw Luke's back stiffen, but he seemed determined not to cause trouble. All he said was, "Excuse me, officer, but I'm in a bit of a hurry."

Graham moved aside, but Hatcher, the other guard, chimed in. "One more thing. If you're so proud of the Klan, why do you cover your heads with a hood?"

For a minute, Geoff thought Luke would lose control and take a swing at Hatcher. Even from the back, the man's tight fists and deep breathing told him he was struggling to control his temper. Apparently, Graham and Hatcher felt it, too, or maybe they realized they had gone too far, because Hatcher settled his right hand on his nightstick. Geoff moved closer,

Gray Love

hoping they weren't about to find themselves with a mess of trouble.

Taking a deep breath to calm down, Luke said quietly, "May I please visit my friend now?"

At a nod from Geoff, both officers stepped politely aside, directing Luke to Ken's jail cell. "Two doors down on your right."

"Thank you, officers."

Luke walked to the place the officers had pointed out, and Geoff wandered past them to the end of the cellblock, where he sat at a desk positioned there. Luke ignored him, looking through the bars at Ken Lewis, who lay on a narrow bed, reading the Bible.

"Hey, Ken." Luke's voice echoed strangely through the hall.

"It's good to see you, Luke." Ken set the Bible aside, rose and moved closer to the bars.

"Why have they arrested you?"

"They're trying to stick me with murder. Can you believe that shit?" Ken sounded genuinely affronted.

"Nope, can't see it. They ain't got no kinda proof, do they?" Luke said, shaking his head. He glanced down the hall both ways before lowering his voice and adding, "Mathew knows you're here. He'll get you out. Just be strong for us, and keep your mouth shut, okay?"

"I'm trying," Ken whined, leaning his face against the bars. "I miss my woman and my cozy bed."

"Just keep cool," Luke said, keeping his voice low. "We'll discuss it at our next meeting and find a way to get you released."

Ken nodded. "Tell Mathew that I ain't gonna say nothin' to nobody, okay?"

"He'll be happy to hear that," Luke replied. They shook hands, and Luke walked past the officers and down the hall, apparently looking for Waldron's office.

Geoff got up to return to his own desk, but stopped close enough to the Chief's office to hear the conversation.

Luke leaned against Chief Waldron's doorway, looking like he had all day to find out what he wanted. The Chief looked up. "Can I help you?"

"How long will Mr. Lewis be here?" Luke asked.

"I don't know." The Chief took off his glasses and laid them on his blotter. "He hasn't been arraigned yet, so I don't know if the judge will post bond or not."

Luke nodded, but didn't say another word. He turned and hurried away, pushing through the outer doors.

Geoff wondered how Luke would break the bad news to the rest of his Klan buddies.

At six p.m., Mathew Stephens dismissed court and headed home. Hannah, on the other hand, was still defending Cecilia Rose, one of her clients who had been accused of assaulting her husband after she found him in their bed with another woman. As she walked back to her table, she noticed Mathew enter the back of the courtroom. She glanced at her watch and smiled. Fifteen minutes later, the judge adjourned the session until the next day.

While Hannah packed up her briefcase, Mathew approached her table and casually leaned against the edge. He was dressed in faded jeans and an open-necked polo shirt. "You did well this evening."

"Thank you," she replied with a smile, closing her briefcase with a snap. He picked it up.

"Are you ready?" he asked.

She nodded and smiled when he held the big wooden door of the courtroom wide so she could pass through. "I ordered some take-out. I hope you like seafood."

She gave him a wink. "I love seafood."

They walked outside to the parking lot.

"My car's over there," he said.

She remembered the dark green BMW that had been parked in his drive, and made her way toward it without prompting. The tan leather seats cuddled her close when he handed her in, and he climbed into the driver's seat, smiling across at her as he shut the door.

"Let's pickup the food, shall we? I'm starving."

At her nod, he started the car and slid smoothly out of the parking lot, blending into the traffic on Main Street without any trouble. Hannah leaned her head against the plush headrest, enjoying the companionable silence and wondering where the evening would take them in what she hesitantly thought of as a relationship – or, at the least, the beginning of one.

After picking up two delicious-smelling sacks from the crab shack, they drove to the marina. Mathew parked his car in the lot.

"Here we are." He indicated the lake with a flourish.

Hannah almost forgot to breathe as she looked out at the glittering expanse of water cradling the setting sun. "It's gorgeous."

"Wait till you see my boat," Mathew said, grinning like a school boy on "show and tell" day.

They walked along the pier to where his boat gently bobbed against the wooden dock, glowing softly white in the twilight. It had a tall deck, complete with a fair-sized wheel, and a tiny room underneath with a miniscule kitchen and a small table that folded out from a wide bunk.

"I know it's small, but it makes me happy," he said as Hannah glanced at the bed and table.

She turned to smile up at him. "I love it."

They sat at the tiny table, and Hannah opened the bags, setting out food and plastic utensils.

"You made a great impression in court tonight," Mathew said sincerely. "Beautiful, intelligent, *and* persuasive. If I were on the jury, I'd want to lock that cheating S.O.B. up and throw away the key. Frankly, I think you'll be able to get her off on the assault charges."

"Thank you. You sound surprised," Hannah said, looking down so that her hair hid the warmth in her cheeks.

"I know it's never polite to ask a woman her age," he said with a smile, "but may I ask how old you are?"

She swallowed a mouthful of shrimp and answered, "I'm thirty-six… and you?"

"Forty-four," he said without hesitation.

Hannah gave a low whistle. "Wow, you don't look it."

"Thank you." Mathew grinned. "I'm not used to such compliments."

Before she could stop herself, Hannah blurted out, "How come?" Given his good looks and charming smile, she believed he wouldn't have a hard time dating any woman he wanted.

He wiped the corner of his mouth with a napkin. "As I said the day we met, between work, the plantation, and everything else, I haven't had much time for dating."

"What a shame," she teased. "You need to take time out for fun once in a while."

He gave her a sly look from beneath slanted brows. "Maybe you could give me some suggestions."

Hannah did something she hadn't done in years. She giggled, scrunched up her nose, and threw her head back. She hadn't had this much fun with a member of the opposite sex in a long time. And she had certainly never felt this comfortable with Kenneth, no matter how much her mother wanted them to end up together. Kenneth was so anxious to date her that she often felt smothered by his presence. Whereas Mathew looked at her in a way no other man ever had. He touched her with such delicacy that her heart beat faster every time she thought about him. Although they hadn't known each other long, she felt confident that Mathew Stephens was her Mr. Right.

Around midnight, Mathew drove her back to the courthouse parking lot to retrieve her vehicle. As Hannah got out of his car, he grabbed her hand and pulled her to him, giving her a sweet, probing kiss. Hannah walked to her car, dizzy from the passion she had shared with him. It had been a soul-baring kiss neither could deny, and the beginning of a love neither were ready to admit. After she got into her car, Mathew drove away with her heart.

Chapter Ten

Thursday morning, Hannah sat at her desk with a stack of old case files. Thoughts of Mathew interrupted her work, so she pulled out a court directory and flipped through the pages.

After two rings, Mathew's secretary answered the phone. "Mathew Stephens' office."

"Judge Stephens, please." Hannah kept her voice brisk and businesslike.

"May I ask who is calling?"

Without pause, Hannah said, "The district attorney." She didn't bother to tell the woman which district or the fact that she wasn't really a district attorney. She wanted to surprise Mathew, and it was only a small white lie. She almost giggled.

"Judge Stephens." Mathew's clipped words made her smile even more.

"Hello, Mathew, it's me. Don't you sound all official?" she joked, picturing him in his black robes, gavel in hand. Yum.

"Hi, sweetheart, what are you doing?" His voice brightened.

As she thought about his boyish smile, it gave her a warm glow inside.

"I was wondering if you liked Chinese and carrot cake."

"Chinese carrot cake? I didn't know there *was* such a thing," Mathew teased.

"No, silly, Chinese food with carrot cake for dessert," she giggled.

"Sure," he replied. "Why?"

"I thought I might come over tonight with some food," she offered persuasively. "Even judges need to eat."

She heard him chuckle, which made her smile even bigger.

Gray Love

"I would love to have you for dinner," he answered in a suggestive tone that gave her chills.

"Great. See you after work," Hannah said. "I have to run."

Hannah hung up, her mind working overtime. There would be lots to do before she saw him tonight. Burying herself in work, the rest of the day flew past in a blur. At five o'clock, she hurried to her car and drove to her favorite bakery, where she purchased a carrot cake before heading home for a hot bath. As she drove home, she mentally reviewed her closet for something sexy and flirty. Her emerald green silk shift and matching Jimmy Choo shoes would fit the bill nicely, if a little dressy for dinner at home.

"Hannah, is that you?" her mother called up the steps.

Hannah rolled her eyes. *Who else would it be?* "Yes, Ma, it's me."

Mrs. Collins walked up the stairs and into Hannah's room, looking at her daughter in amazement.

"What are you trying to do, make the gentleman's eyeballs pop out?"

Hannah smiled, twirling to show off the effect of her outfit. Then she asked, "Can you do me a favor and order two sweet and sour chicken take-out dinners from the Panda?"

Her mother frowned in disapproval. "You're so wrong to bring that man take-out, but I'll call it in."

Hannah finished dressing, and joined her mother downstairs in the kitchen. Deborah's eyes grew moist, and she clasped her hands together over her bosom.

"Oh, Hannah, you are so beautiful. I've never seen you look so happy."

Hannah moved around the table to hug her mother. "Thanks, Ma."

"I ordered your food," her mother said, brushing at her tears. "I really would love to meet the gentleman who is making you blossom like a spring flower."

"I'll see what I can do," Hannah said, wishing her parents would stop asking, although she knew they were only concerned for her welfare. "Gotta run, kiss Daddy for me."

"I will, dear. Have a good time."

Hannah walked out the door with the carrot cake and drove to the Panda to pick up her take-out order.

At Mathew's house, she parked in the driveway and walked up his front steps, juggling two bags and the cake. She rang the doorbell with her elbow.

Mathew's face lit up with a broad smile when he opened the door. "You really came." He seemed pleased, if a little surprised.

"I said I would, didn't I?" She nodded toward the food in her arms. "Give me a hand?"

She handed him the cake, which he gingerly took, holding it like a newborn baby. She giggled and stepped past him and into the foyer.

"What's all this?" he asked.

She laughed at his apparent memory loss. Had she really gotten under his skin so much?

"I said I was bringing dinner. Don't you remember?"

"That's right. You were bringing Chinese carrot cake." He chuckled before turning serious. "You went to so much trouble. Thank you."

"No problem."

As he led the way to the formal dining room, she was still awed over the splendor of his home.

Mathew placed the food on the dining room table, and approached Hannah as she stood in the doorway, giving her a head-to-foot appraisal.

"You look incredible." He looked down at his khaki slacks and button-down shirt. "I just got home from work, but I did bathe."

"Well, it's such a relief to know you have excellent hygiene," Hanna laughed. "It seems like every time I see you, you have just taken a bath."

For a moment, they stared at each other as if they couldn't get their fill.

Mathew finally broke the spell. "I have just the thing to go with this." Heading in to the kitchen, he opened the frig, retrieved a bottle of Chardonnay, grabbed two crystal wine glasses from the cupboard, and carried them into the dining room. "Let's eat. I'm starving."

"Good idea." She brushed past him with a teasing touch.

While they ate, Hannah noticed Mathew staring at her. When her eyes met his gaze, he asked, "Where do you live?"

"Not far from here," she replied. "I'm single, but I've been saving for a down payment on a house, so I still live at home with my parents."

"There's nothing wrong with that." He smiled, his glance sweeping the room. "This is my parents' house... or I should say was. After Daddy retired, my mother wanted to travel the world. They fell in love with a villa in Southern England and bought it. So I sold my bachelor pad and moved back home."

She followed his gaze, past the open door to the large kitchen. This house had been built for children, preferably a large family. "You live here alone?"

"Yep, just me, myself, and I. This was my family's plantation," he said proudly. "My father had twelve Negroes working his fields and three house Negroes."

Hannah tried to picture it, but couldn't. "And what about now? Who helps with your land?"

"I employ four Negroes now." He lowered his gaze to his food, as if afraid to look at her.

"Do they have to be black?" she asked.

"I prefer it that way. I like to keep tradition."

Hannah shifted in her chair, an uncomfortable tightness in her chest.

As if realizing what he had said, Mathew apologized for his remarks. "I'm sorry. I didn't mean it like that. I just think blacks work harder."

"Or do you mean that black people are cheaper to employ?" Hannah said in a sarcastic voice.

"No, that's not what I meant." Mathew shook his head.

She plucked the napkin from her lap and dropped it on the table. Suddenly, the food tasted more like sawdust than Chinese. "Just what did you mean? You act like you're still living back in the nineteenth century. That slave mentality just won't cut it any longer. Don't you know that things... people have changed?"

"I guess not," he replied. With a charming smile, he added, "Can you forgive me?"

She nodded reluctantly.

"I've never known a black woman as beautiful and intelligent as you," he said.

"It's the twenty-first century. You should get out in the real world more often," she retorted.

"Yes, I suppose I should," he laughed.

"So are you saying I'm beautiful?" Her tense fingers relaxed a little. She should give him the benefit of the doubt; maybe she was being too sensitive. Surely, he hadn't meant any harm. Maybe he just didn't know any better.

Warm color suffused his cheeks. "More beautiful than any woman I have ever known."

In spite of her misgivings, Hannah felt a small thrill of joy and excitement course through her.

When they finished eating, Hannah tossed the containers in the large steel trashcan near the back door and set the rest of the cake on the counter. Mathew followed her to the kitchen and helped her clean up. Then he took her by the hand and led her into the living room. Sitting close together on the sofa, he placed an arm around her shoulders and lightly stroked her cheek with his fingers. Hannah slid off her pumps, tucked her feet against the back of the sofa, and snuggled against him.

"Has anyone ever told you how lovely you are?" he breathed against her ear. "Or how soft your skin is?"

Hannah leaned toward him, intoxicated with his closeness, yet she tried for a note of humor to lighten the mood. "You're not so bad yourself."

As if he had been waiting for her to speak, Mathew moved closer and pressed his lips against hers with a groan. Hannah returned the kiss, reveling in the sweet passion of his lips as they sank deeper into the sofa cushions. Her skin tingled wherever he touched her, leaving a burning trail of fire along her face, neck, and arms. She sighed as his lips brushed her cheek and lingered in the curve of her neck, and when Mathew moved, she felt his urgent need for her. Hannah wanted him, too, more than any man she had ever known.

"Mathew, wait," she whispered. "I don't know if this is right. I haven't done this in a long time."

He rose up and looked into her eyes, a gentle smile on his lips. "It's been awhile for me, too," he reassured her. "I'll be careful."

Hannah didn't want to think, worry, or do anything but feel as he kissed and stroked her body, so she nodded slowly. He closed his eyes and lowered his mouth to hers once more, and she lost herself in the passion of his kiss.

She pulled his shirt out of his pants with eager hands, and guided his hands to the zipper holding her dress together. Hannah wanted him so badly she couldn't wait. His skin felt warm, firm, and soft at the same time, and it drove her crazy. She wanted to caress his hard muscular body and flat stomach with nothing between them.

The zipper opened, and he slowly slid the dress past her shoulders to her waist. His indrawn breath made her glad she had decided against a bra today, and when his lips and tongue found one of her taut nipples, she moaned, arching against him, lost to everything except the feel, the taste, and the aching need for him.

She quickly unbuttoned his shirt and tossed it aside, wanting... needing more.

Mathew groaned as he moved against her, the hard length of his erection pressed firmly against her belly as he reached up to kiss her again. Hannah guided his hands as he pushed her dress down over her hips and thighs to land unceremoniously on the polished wooden floor.

"I want you, Mathew," Hannah breathed against his neck. "Please... hurry."

She didn't care about anything but fulfilling the burning need inside her, the wonder of his passion, and feeling the hardness of his body inside hers. She didn't care if it hurt or what anyone thought. Hannah knew that she loved him, and she wanted him to know it, too.

At her urging, Mathew hooked his fingers into the sides of her lace panties and gently pulled them off, dropping them next to her dress as he planted soft butterfly kisses across her belly, driving her insane with need. She pushed his shirt off his shoulders, and it joined the growing pile on the floor. Reaching for his belt buckle, she fumbled with the fastenings on his trousers until he gently pushed her fingers aside. In seconds, he was free of his remaining clothing, and her arms drew him back to her,

Mathew didn't hesitate. He pressed his burning flesh against hers, capturing her lips in a fevered kiss as his hands parted her silken thighs and he slid into her warmth with one smooth stroke. Hannah gasped into his mouth as he filled her, pressing her down against the sofa cushions. He stopped, still deep within her, and drew his mouth away, but she drew her legs up and tightened them around his hips, frantically urging him on. At her touch, he moaned softly, nuzzling against her neck as his hips began to move, building a steady rhythm of desire. Hannah pushed upward, matching him stroke for stroke, kissing every inch of skin she could reach, her nails curled into his back as he cried out against her, matching her own cries of ecstasy as they reached the pinnacle of desire.

An hour later, they were still cuddled together on the sofa. Hannah knew this was the man she wanted to spend the rest of her life with… the man who would make her happy. And she wouldn't allow anything to spoil this feeling.

Chapter Eleven

Mathew held her close, wondering how someone could be so beautiful, so perfect. Yet, the fact that she was a black woman went against everything he had ever believed in. Following that thought came another, more urgent one. He loved Hannah, had loved her since the day he had first seen her swimming across his lake. Yet, how could this be possible? His long-held beliefs and his own activities had brought him to this state of confusion. How could he possibly be in love with Hannah Collins?

She shifted against him, and he looked down at her softly smiling face as she snuggled against him on the sofa. He had drawn an afghan over them as their bodies cooled from heated lovemaking. Hannah eyes glittered with tears.

He drew a gentle fingertip across her cheek. "Why are you crying?"

She smiled and tenderly brushed his hand aside. "I'm just happy."

"Happy?" he joked. "This is how you show me you're happy?"

She lowered her eyes and a wash of color slid up her neck to her cheeks. "I've never felt this way, Mathew. I didn't know it could be like this."

Her large brown eyes fastened on his face, as she waited to hear the right answer to her question.

Mathew leaned down to kiss her, then murmured against her cheek, "You were wonderful, Hannah. More like perfect."

He drew away to watch her expression. Her beaming smile assured him that she felt the same earth-shattering passion that still held him captive. Mathew hugged her close.

"So, where do we go from here?"

"You know, my parents have been in my face for the past two days," she said teasingly, running her fingers along his right shoulder and down to his chest. "They want to know all about you."

"Really?" He seemed surprised. "I would be happy to meet them, if you want me to."

"Are you sure?" She leaned back to look deeply into his eyes. "I know we're not serious or anything yet."

"I want to see you more often," he said, dropping a kiss on her pert little nose. "We've been together for so short a time, and yet, I feel as though we've known each other for a lifetime. And there's nothing I would like better than to meet your folks."

She smiled. "Will you come for dinner on Saturday?"

Mathew nodded, smoothing a strand of dark hair from her damp forehead. "I would be honored."

"Good," she said. "I'll pick you up at five."

"Okay." Mathew kissed her again. "Hannah, I have to ask you something. You don't feel uncomfortable dating a white man, do you?"

Hannah shook her head. "Why should I?"

"I don't know," he said with a grimace. "Your people won't... object?"

"No," she replied, laughing at his wording. "Will *your* people mind?"

Mathew didn't know how to answer that. His people? The only people he had left were his parents and the Klan, and yes, they would mind. They would mind a whole lot. Watching

Hannah's trusting face, he forced another smile. "I don't think so," he lied, and immediately felt guilty.

She relaxed against him, as if his answer meant a lot, and suddenly, he was ashamed of his part in the Klan. He had believed in what he was doing for so long, he didn't know how to let go. The only thing he was sure of was that he wanted to be with Hannah, and that would never be tolerated. Oddly enough, once his parents got to know how beautiful and smart Hannah was and how much he loved her, he believed they would accept her. But the Klan was another story. Something would have to be done to show them that they were wrong. The Klan had been killing folks, based purely on skin color. Never realizing that black, white, red, or yellow, people were all a part of one race, the human race and were very much alike.

All this time they had spent hating each others' differences, and now Mathew knew from the bottom of his soul that they had been so very wrong. Filled with vengeance and injustice, they had completely lost the meaning of what real justice was. Mankind included all humans, regardless of the color of their skin.

Hannah moved restlessly. "It's late. I have to go," she said reluctantly.

"I wish you could spend the night." The words left his mouth before he had even finished forming the thought.

"Me, too," she murmured. "Maybe tomorrow?" She looked at him hopefully.

"Tomorrow works," he said with a grin. "Besides, it's Friday, so we can stay up later." He wiggled his eyebrows suggestively, and she laughed happily.

"Sounds great," she said, sitting up on the sofa and reaching for her clothes.

Within minutes, they were walking to the front door, and Mathew opened it for her, leaning down to kiss her.

"I'll miss you," he whispered against her lips.

She smiled. "See you tomorrow."

He pulled her close for one more kiss before walking Hannah to her car. She reached for his hand, and he folded his warm fingers around hers, enjoying their closeness. At the car, she stopped, and he opened the door.

"I had a wonderful time."

"Me, too," he replied.

He waved as she drove away, and then went back inside, moving through the house, turning off lights and locking up before climbing the wide staircase to the upper floor. As he got ready for bed, Mathew thought about the Klan and the men, his friends, who looked to him for guidance in their mission of hate, and he knew he would have to choose between them and Hannah.

Hannah was important to him. Even though he had only known her a short time. She seemed to complete him, make him whole, and his world better. How could he choose someone he had only known for a few days over friends he had known for years?

As he lay in bed, the question swirled in his mind, along with images of burning crosses and the screams of dying men. If she knew what he had done, she would hate him, and Mathew realized he desperately wanted Hannah's love.

Chapter Twelve

Friday morning dawned bright and early. Hannah lazily stretched, feeling the strain of muscles unused for a long time. Mathew. The thought of him brought a smile to her lips. Could this man really be the one? She rolled over, luxuriating in the feel of her naked skin beneath the sheets. When she had fallen into bed last night, she had wanted nothing to mask the memory of his touch.

Noises downstairs reminded her that today was another workday, and she reluctantly got up, dressed for court, and headed downstairs to join her parents for breakfast.

"Good morning, Ma, Dad."

She sat down at the kitchen table and reached for a glass of grapefruit juice.

"How was your date last night?" her mother asked.

"It was wonderful." Hannah took a bite of toast, trying not to blush. She quickly changed the subject. "By the way, Mathew has agreed to come to dinner Saturday."

"Oh, that's wonderful, dear." Deborah Collins clapped her hands. "He can enjoy a real meal instead of take-out. What should I make?"

"Whatever you decide will be great," Hannah laughed.

Her mother got up, hurried over to her recipe box, and started rummaging through it.

Hannah's father looked up and winked. "Your Mother will be planning this meal for the rest of the day."

Hannah rose from her chair, and leaned down to kiss the top of her father's balding head.

"I'll see you guys later this evening," she said, glancing at her watch.

"Okay, dear, have a nice day," her father called to her retreating back.

Hannah hurried out the door before her mother could comment that she had eaten only a bite or two of food. There was only one thing she was hungry for now, one person. She couldn't wait to see Mathew again.

* * *

After due consideration, Mathew decided to call Chief Waldron to see if he could find out what they had on Ken Lewis.

"Chief, this is Judge Mathew Stephens," he said when Waldron answered the phone.

"Good morning, Judge Stephens. How are you this morning?"

"I'm doing fine, how about you?" Mathew asked, almost as an afterthought. He blinked rapidly, trying to focus on what he needed to do, but the thought of Hannah's soft skin and tender lips kept distracting him.

"Good. It's been a long time since we talked," Waldron said. "What can I do for you?"

Mathew wondered how much the Chief knew about Lewis and the Klan. He cleared his throat. "I'm calling about Ken Lewis."

There was a moment of silence. "Oh, you mean the Klan man," the Chief replied.

Mathew let the comment go and continued. "Some friends of his came by my courtroom yesterday, asking about him."

Another moment of silence passed.

"Do you know what charges have been filed against Mr. Lewis?" the Chief asked gruffly.

"All I was told was that he had been arrested." Mathew decided to play it safe. He wasn't going to admit anything, hoping that the Chief would tell him what they knew.

Waldron's words were clipped. "We believe that he was allegedly involved in the murder of Taylor Henderson."

"From what his friends say, I think that is highly unlikely," Mathew tried to sound reasonable, but his heart raced. If they had linked Ken to the crime, he might be coerced to spill his guts about the rest of them. And if it that happened, Hannah would find out that he had not only lied to her, but was one of those who hated people who were different from himself.

"I appreciate your sentiments," the Chief said, "but we have enough evidence to support the arrest."

"I understand," Mathew said. "Well, good luck in your investigation, Chief, and please keep me posted."

* * *

Danny Pummel got ready for work while Connie made breakfast. When he finished dressing, he joined her in the kitchen.

"Sit down," she said. "Breakfast is almost ready."

He gave her a quick kiss on the cheek, wrapping his arms around her from behind. She grew quiet for a moment.

"Honey, I don't like you being involved with the KKK," she said finally.

"I know you don't, but someone has to uncover them." He squeezed her a little tighter.

She shrugged him off, motioning him to sit at the table while she scooped scrambled eggs and grits onto a warm plate. "I know, but why can't it be someone else?"

"It has to be someone the Klan will accept," Danny patiently explained, watching as she arranged toast and sliced strawberries on his plate. "As an undercover detective, I fit the bill."

"I'm worried about you, honey," she said, looking over her shoulder, her eyes tearing up. "I'm worried about being here alone when you're gone at night."

"Honey, you don't have to worry. Come here." Danny patted his knee, and Connie carried his plate to the table and settled herself in his lap. Danny slid his arms around her. "I'm not going to let anyone hurt you," he said earnestly. "And I'm not going to get hurt. I promise. I'll be very careful." He lifted her chin, raising her gaze to his. "Okay?"

She nodded, a trembling smile struggling to reach her lips. "Okay."

Danny pulled her closer. "I love you, and nothing's going to happen to me. You have my word on it."

Connie gave him a kiss and pushed out of his lap to fetch her own plate. "Just remember, you don't break your promises."

Danny smiled. "That's right. I don't." He grabbed her as she passed; snatching her plate of food, he set it on the table so he could pull her back into his lap. He kissed on the lips. "You're still as gorgeous as you were the day you walked down the aisle fifteen years ago."

Connie leaned into him, tracing a finger along his strong jaw. "Why don't we have a little fun this evening? We need to keep practicing, if we're going to make a baby," she teased.

"Mmm," he murmured, "Sounds good to me."

"Okay then. Eat and get out of here so I can get something done before you come home tonight," she ordered, getting up to move over to her chair.

Danny dug into his grits, toast and eggs. By the time he was ready to leave, Connie had calmed down and was puttering around the kitchen, doing dishes and setting out frozen steaks for dinner. With a kiss, she hurried him out the door to work.

Geoff and the Chief were already seated in Waldron's office, waiting for him.

"About time you showed up," Waldron said, glancing at his clock with a grin. "It's quarter after ten."

"I overslept," Danny said as he slid into a chair next to Geoff. "What's going on?"

The Chief picked up his pencil and tapped it against his upper lip, watching Danny. "We're going to arrest whoever comes to the meeting Sunday. You up for it?"

"I just want to get this over with," Danny said, running a hand through his hair in frustration.

Geoff nodded his understanding.

"What time is the meeting?" Waldron asked.

"It's at eight," Danny replied. "Most of them leave by ten, so you'll want to be there by nine o'clock."

The Chief smiled grimly. "Nine o'clock it is. Make sure you're strapped and protected, you hear?"

"I never go undercover without protection." Danny patted his unprotected chest.

"Good. What else do you need to know?" The Chief dropped his pencil and leaned back in his chair, eyeing Danny across its cluttered surface.

"How many men are you bringing?"

"We're going in with twenty-five officers," Waldron said quietly, as if he knew and appreciated Danny's concern. "You don't have anything to worry about."

"Okay, Chief, I'm counting on you."

Waldron pulled a folder toward him from a pile on his desk. "Tomorrow morning, there will be a meeting with the participating officers, so we can get everything coordinated."

"What time?" Geoff asked.

"Eight o'clock sharp. I want both of you to be here." Chief Waldron glared at them from beneath bushy brows. "I've been trying to bust the Klan in Crystal Springs for a long time, and I'll be damned if I'm going to let this golden opportunity pass."

They spent the remainder of the day planning the raid. Everyone was excited that the KKK reign of terror might finally be coming to an end.

Geoff worried about the Sunday raid all the way home, exploring what could go wrong in his mind. His hands tightened on the wheel. He wasn't going to let anything happen to Danny or any of his co-workers and friends on the force.

Rosie was cooking dinner, and he smelled the tantalizing odor of tomatoes and basil as soon as he entered the house.

"Rosie, I'm home," he shouted, dropping his jacket and keys on the table just inside the front door.

"I'm in the kitchen," she called.

He joined her, leaning over to give her a quick hug and a peck on the cheek. "Boy am I glad to be home. Mmm that smells good."

"Did you have a hard day today?"

"Uh huh."

"Sorry about that, sweetheart," Rosie said. "I'm cooking steak and pasta. Dinner will be ready in a jiffy. Why don't you freshen up first?"

He trudged up the stairs, ready for a hot shower and some of his wife's excellent cooking, wondering what Rosie would do if anything ever happened to him. As he stood under the spray of heated water, he thought about what it would feel like to lose her forever and knew he wasn't ready to die. He had to win this fight. When he finished showering, he pulled on a pair of jeans and a T-shirt, and made his way back downstairs.

"You look beat," Rosie said when he walked into the kitchen.

"I am," he said, pulling a chair out from under the table. "I think I'm more emotionally exhausted than anything. We have so much to do tomorrow. It's unreal."

"Here, help me with this." She handed him two plates with matching silverware, and he set their places at the table while she put the finishing touches on dinner. Bringing the skillet over to the table, she placed a steak on each plate – well done on hers and medium rare on his. She returned with a bowl of tomato, garlic and basil pasta and set it between them on the tabletop, then dropped into the chair opposite his.

With a smile, she reached for his hand, and they prayed, thanking God for the meal, for safely bringing Rosie's mother through some minor surgery, and for protecting Geoff and his fellow officers. When they finished praying, they dug into the food. She glanced across the table at her husband as she ladled a heaping spoonful of noodles on her plate.

"How's the Henderson case coming?"

"We're planning to arrest the remaining KKK members at a meeting Sunday night," he answered, concentrating on cutting his steak so she wouldn't see his eyes. "Danny has gotten enough information that we can bring them in for questioning."

"Is Danny doing okay?" she asked.

"He's all right, I guess. I'm worried about him, though. Once the Klan finds out you've betrayed them, that's it." He finally glanced up at her, keeping his expression calm.

She shook her head. "Poor Connie must be worried sick."

"Yes, of course," Geoff nodded, glad to see she hadn't focused on what might happen to him. "When isn't she worried?"

* * *

Usually, the muted oak paneling and soft blue walls of his office helped Mathew relax. Today, as he sat and pondered his situation, calm was a million miles away. He loved Hannah, and all he could think about these days were her soft feminine curves and tender kisses. Although the words had never passed either of their lips, he believed she felt the same way about him.

He wanted to celebrate their love, and yet, his Klansmen – the men he shared more memories with than his own family – would not understand. If they found out about his relationship with Hannah, they would turn against him, unless he handled things just right. Should he call Sunday's meeting off to buy more time? The question whirled around in his mind like a two-bit rollercoaster ride at an amusement park.

The Klan was only half the problem. If Hannah ever found out about his involvement with them, it would destroy their relationship and ruin any chance they might have of a future together. What excuse could he possibly offer, if she found out? "Oh, I'm sorry, I used to hate black people, but I do love you." How could he even call it a relationship under those circumstances?

Mathew finally decided to phone Reverend Butler and tell him to switch this week's meeting to his house. Later, he would make up some excuse as to why he wasn't able to attend this week.

He punched the number into his phone and listened to the ringing.

"Hello."

"Reverend Butler?"

"Yes."

"Mathew Stephens."

"How are you?" the Reverend asked.

"I'm fine. You?"

"I'm doing well," Butler replied. "What can I do for you?"

"Well, Reverend, I've decided to move the meeting to your house this Sunday."

"My house? Why?"

Mathew hadn't realized that he would have to explain why he couldn't have the meeting at his place. "Well, I'm doing a little renovating, and everything is a mess…" he began.

"No need to explain. Is the meeting still on for eight?"

"Yes, it is," Mathew replied.

"Sounds good," the Reverend said. "I'll let the guys know."

Chapter Thirteen

Danny strolled through the police station doors the next morning and found Geoff talking to the Chief in his office.

"There's been a change in plans," he said, moving past Geoff to drop into one of the chairs in front of the Chief's desk.

"What do you mean?" Waldron looked up from the papers on his desk.

"The meeting has been moved to Reverend Butler's home."

"Why the sudden change in plans?" Geoff looked puzzled. "Do you think they suspect something?"

"I doubt it," Danny replied.

"Did the judge sound worried on the phone, Chief?" Geoff asked.

"No, he played it pretty cool," Waldron replied.

"It doesn't matter where the Klan has the meeting as long as they all show up," Danny said.

"We'll have to notify the task force at the briefing so they'll know where to be Sunday," the Chief said.

"I'll take care of it," Geoff said.

"How are you holding up, Danny?" Waldron asked.

The detective shifted uncomfortably and gazed at his superior with troubled eyes. "I just want this to be over with. This case has gotten under my skin, and I feel like I'm betraying some of those men who will be there Sunday. Some of them may be murderers, but the ones who aren't could have been friends."

"You're not betraying anyone," Geoff said. "The Klan has murdered people for years... all of them, whether they actually pulled the trigger or not."

"I know," Danny muttered. "I just don't understand how they can do the things they do and not feel some kind of guilt."

"That's what makes you a good man, my friend," Geoff replied as he got to his feet. "Once this is over, you won't have to worry about it ever again."

"You're right." Danny nodded. "I just don't want anyone to get hurt."

Geoff nodded, leaning down to pat Danny's shoulder. "I know you don't, but you know how these things go. Stopping them may result in someone being hurt, but it's their call. They can either be arrested peacefully, or they can put of a fight. Either way, there isn't much we can do about it."

Danny lowered his head for a moment, then sighed and followed Geoff out of the room.

* * *

Hannah finished her cases by noon, and decided to leave work early.

"Monica," she told her secretary, "if anyone calls or comes in, I'll be in Monday morning."

"Yes, ma'am," Monica replied with a smile. Hannah hummed as she got ready to leave, tidying up her desk and putting her files away. As she stepped back into the outer office, Monica grinned at her.

"Miss Collins? I can't help but notice how happy you've been the last couple days. Is there something… or someone new in your life?"

Hannah winked at her, and waved good-bye without answering. Actually, she had been a lot happier since she had met Mathew, and she wondered who else besides Monica had noticed. Today she wanted to go home and spend a little extra time getting ready for her date.

Gray Love

She parked on her side of the driveway and made her way to the kitchen door. Nobody used the front door in her mother's house. Her mother's kitchen lay at the heart of their home, where family and friends gathered for food and conversation, sometimes even a little music when her Daddy brought out his fiddle, and Uncle Ray played the guitar. As she expected, her mother moved back and forth between the sink and the refrigerator, preparing supper.

"You're home early," her mother remarked.

Hannah gave her mother a hug. "Yep," she agreed. "I decided to come home and relax before my date."

Mrs. Collins smiled at her daughter, reaching up to smooth a strand of dark hair from Hannah's forehead. "I can't wait to meet the man who makes you so happy that you leave work early."

"You'll like him," Hannah assured her, turning to head upstairs. "I think Daddy will, too."

Hannah took a hot shower, and picked out a pair of tight blue jeans and a low-cut sleeveless top of ivory silk to show off the creamy tan of her skin. A pair of ivory, strapped sandals completed the outfit. As she sat down at her makeup table, her mother came in.

"Darling, I want you to be careful." Mrs. Collins settled on the edge of the bed, watching her daughter apply eyeliner.

"Mother, please," Hannah said. "I'm thirty-six years old."

Her mother tilted her head to one side, a worried expression marring her pretty features. "The Klan is after your daddy, girl. Them people snatch up loved ones just to prove a point."

"I'm going to be with Mathew," Hannah said adamantly, looking in the mirror to sweep mascara across her long lashes. "I feel safe with him. He won't let anything happen to me."

"I'm probably just being an old woman," her mother said, smiling. "But I am not about to stop worrying about you just because you're not a child any longer. I'm happy you have finally found someone. Your Father and I can't wait to meet him."

"Thanks, Ma." Hannah took the pearl necklace her parents had given her for her sixteenth birthday from her jewelry box and her mother hurried over to help her put it on. She laid a hand on her daughter's shoulder.

Hannah covered her mother's hand with one of her own, reassuring her, "I'll be fine, Ma.

Don't worry so much."

"I can't help it," her mother said with a shaky laugh. "It's my job."

Hannah glanced at herself in the mirror one last time, then picked up her purse and rose to kiss her mother on her soft cheek.

"I've got to get going," she whispered, and headed downstairs and out the front door.

Mathew greeted her from his porch at precisely six o'clock. He smiled when she stepped out of her car.

"You're waiting for me," she teased. "I'm impressed."

He escorted her inside. He was dressed in casual black Dockers and a fitted black shirt that emphasized his athletic build.

She stopped just inside the foyer and studied him as he closed the door. "You look very nice this evening," she complimented him with a sincere smile.

"Why, thank you, ma'am." He gave her a dashing bow before leading her into the dining room.

When she stepped into the room, she gasped in surprise. There was food on the table, a lace tablecloth, two white candles in tall brass candlesticks, and a vase of gorgeous Peace roses.

"It's beautiful," she whispered, walking toward the table to get a better look. The china plates held roasted Cornish hens, with side dishes of cornbread, peach cobbler, and green beans. Two glasses of white wine sparkled in crystal flutes.

"Mathew, how sweet." Hannah turned in his arms and gave him a passionate kiss.

Mathew held her close, smoothing her hair back from her face.

"Let's eat," he whispered in her ear.

They enjoyed lighthearted conversation as they ate. She talked about work and her family, but she noticed that he only spoke of work.

"I know so little about you," she said.

"What else do you want to know?" he asked.

"Well, I know your name is Mathew Stephens, you're forty-four, and you're a judge," she answered, leaning over to touch his cheek. "Is there anything else I should know?"

Shaking his head, he took her hand and led her into the living room, pulling her down on the sofa beside him.

"What would you like to do tonight?" He slid an arm around her shoulders, and she snuggled against his warmth.

She thought for a few moments. "We can go dancing. I know a great club."

"I don't think that's a good idea," Mathew quickly responded.

Hannah shrugged off his response. "Fine. Do you have a CD player?"

"Yes, why?" He looked puzzled.

"I brought some CDs we can to dance to." She smiled at him, standing to pull him up off the couch. "Show me."

He led her to the CD player hidden in an antique mahogany cabinet and opened it with a flourish.

"Will this work?" he grinned.

"Oh, I think it'll do." She turned it on and put in a Keith Sweat CD, selecting a track. She stepped away from the cabinet, waiting for the music to start.

"The name of this song is *Twisted*," she told him, and as the song began to play, she began dancing in front of him.

Hannah stepped seductively closer, and then danced away, teasing him with the sensuous rhythm of her movements. He reached for her, and she slipped away, but came back almost immediately to slide her arms around his neck. When the tempo of the melody increased, she pressed her lower body tightly against his, and he took hold of her waist, pulling her to him.

She saw the look in his eyes, wonder and tenderness edged with the hardness of passion and lust, and it ignited her hunger for him. With a soft moan, she settled against his body, swaying to the pulsing sound beating around them with insistent fervor. He gently kissed her neck, and his hands slipped up her body to fondle her firm breasts. Hannah's nipples hardened at the touch, and she moaned again, finding his mouth with her own. Before the song ended, he picked her up and carried her upstairs to his bedroom, falling with her onto the soft bed.

Impatiently, they struggled with their clothing, throwing the offending articles across the room as soon as they were removed. His tongue burned across her naked shoulder, up her neck, and traced the softness of her lips before claiming them in a searing kiss.

Their bodies moved together as if they were part of the same being, the notes of the music below a counterpoint to each thrust and groan. She wrapped her legs around his thighs and whispered pleasured cries against his heated skin. He strained above her, his eyes closed as he murmured her name over and over again before they exploded together in total surrender.

Later, while they lay in bed talking, Hannah finally looked around the room, admiring the antique furniture and ornate light

Gray Love

fixtures. She snuggled against his chest, breathing in the smell of him, musky and exciting. Her gaze fell on a picture on the nightstand of Mathew surrounded by a group of men, all smiling in camaraderie.

"Wow, look at all those men," she teased. "Are you all in some kind of club?"

"That's just some old buddies of mine at a get-together," he muttered. "It's nothing really, just a picture." He stroked his hand down her naked back. "You're staying the night, aren't you?"

"I'd love to," she accepted, reaching up to kiss him. "And by the way, my parents can't wait to meet you tomorrow."

His expression softened. "I can't wait to meet them either."

His arms tightened around her, and she nuzzled his broad chest, content just to be in his arms for the moment. Tomorrow, she would introduce him to her family and hope for the best. If they understood how she felt about Mathew, his race shouldn't matter, because it didn't matter to her.

She sighed.

"I'm going to shower," she said, wriggling away from him and climbing out of the bed. "Be right back."

Mathew smiled as she walked past him toward the bathroom, her naked skin glowing softly in the darkness of the room.

At the door, she paused. "Care to join me?"

Mathew looked shocked for a second. Then with a grin, he jumped out of bed and followed her into the spacious bathroom.

She leaned in to start the water and, after a moment, stepped into the shower, letting the spray run down her skin before she closed the clouded glass door. She knew he was standing at the door watching as the water caressed her body.

"Well, are you going to just stand there?" she said, lathering her hair with his herbal shampoo.

Without another thought, he joined her, slipping in behind her as she rinsed her hair and lathered liquid soap over her breasts. Mathew reached around to touch them, gently kneading her wet sensitive skin until his fingers found her tight nipples. She whimpered and leaned back against him as he gently teased them. At the sound, he turned her to face him, planting fiery kisses on her neck, cheeks, forehead, nose, and finally her lips as he pressed his throbbing hardness against her stomach. Hannah returned the kiss, crushing her breasts against his chest, the soap making both their bodies' slick. Then Mathew slipped his hands under her firm buttocks and lifted so that she could wrap her legs around his waist as he entered her. They made love slowly this time as the hot water showered down upon them.

* * *

The next morning Hannah woke before Mathew, and decided to make breakfast. Slipping on his silk robe, she walked downstairs and found four black men standing in the kitchen talking. The men grew quiet when they saw her.

"Who are you?" she asked, tightening the belt of the robe.

"We work for Master Stephens," one of the men replied.

"*Master* Stephens?" Hannah raised her eyebrows, taking in the faded jeans and sweat-brimmed hats they wore. As if her glance reminded them, they slipped off their hats.

The one, who had spoken, met her gaze squarely, his broad shoulders tense under the thin white T-shirt. "Yes, we work his fields."

"Do you have names?" she asked, leaning back against the doorway.

"I'm Jimmy," he replied. "His name is Jerry, he's Keenan, and that's Jared." He pointed to each of the men who nodded in succession.

"Nice to meet you," Hannah said with a smile.

"Are you the new cook?" Jimmy asked. He seemed to be the spokesperson of the group.

"I'm Hannah," she replied. "I'm his…"

"Girlfriend," Mathew interrupted from behind her. He had pulled on the Dockers he had worn yesterday before coming downstairs.

"Good morning," she said with a bright smile, not wanting him to know how under dressed she felt for this conversation.

Mathew leaned down to kiss her on the cheek. Then looking at Jimmy, he said, "Shouldn't you guys be working instead of bothering this pretty lady?"

The men with Jimmy lowered their eyes to the floor, saying nothing.

"They're fine, really," Hannah said, trying to lighten the tension in the room.

The men walked outside, and Hannah watched as they disappeared around the side of the house. She turned to Mathew with a stunned look. "They call you master? They act like slaves."

"I guess that's pretty formal," Mathew said in a serious tone.

"Yes, master." Hannah joked, but in the back of her mind, she wondered about the strange situation.

Mathew frowned, as if he felt her discomfort, but before he could say anything, she glanced up at the clock.

"I need to get going," she said. "Don't forget about dinner. I'll pick you up at five."

Mathew nodded, reaching out to pull her close. "Leaving so early? I'll miss you until then," he teased, his lips against her hair.

"I want to go home and help my mother with dinner and the house, so we'll be ready." With a quick kiss, she left him, running upstairs to get dressed. Five minutes later, she came down and gave him a long hug.

"I'll finish dressing and walk you outside," Mathew said.

"It's okay. I'm fine," she assured him, reaching up to kiss his cheek in appreciation of the gentlemanly offer. "I'll see you tonight."

With that, she headed out the door. As she walked to her car, she noticed the four men working the fields. As she passed, Jimmy raised a hand to wave before turning back to his work. She pictured them looking like slaves of the past, working on the old plantation, and envisioned "Master" Mathew riding out on a big black horse to inspect their work, lashing his whip against their backs if he disapproved. So what would that make her?

The thought sent a shiver up her bare arms as she got into the car and left.

Chapter Fourteen

When she arrived home, Hannah hurried up the back steps and into the sunny kitchen. Her mother sat reading the morning newspaper at the small table, a vase with a dozen white roses almost obscuring her from view.

"Good morning, Ma," she said breathlessly, laying her purse on the kitchen counter.

"Girl, where have you been?" Mrs. Collins asked.

Hannah felt a tide of warmth rise from her neck to her cheeks. "I was with Mathew. I'm sorry. I should have called."

Her mother frowned, her soft brown eyes disapproving. "Kenneth Williams came by yesterday at seven-thirty looking for you. He brought you those flowers." She pointed to the vase of roses.

Hannah slapped her hand to her forehead. "Oh no, I completely forgot."

"What did you forget?" her mother asked.

"I was supposed to go out with him."

"You're really hung up on this Mathew fellow." Her mother's expression softened a little. "Is he still coming for dinner tonight?"

"I'm picking him up at five," Hannah replied.

Her mother got up from the table. "Good. Your father can't wait to meet him."

"I'm going to change, and then I'll come down and help get ready, okay?"

At her mother's nod, Hannah danced upstairs to change and think about her night with Mathew. She never thought she could be swept off her feet and carried with such love-filled bliss.

Even though she knew Mathew's race would shock her parents, she couldn't wait for them to meet him. The thought of him officially becoming a part of her life made her heart race.

When she thought about his workers, however, her happiness dimmed. Mathew employed only black men. Was it because he wanted to pretend he owned slaves? Did the thought amuse him, or only add fuel to the rumors she had heard of his KKK activities? Hannah shook her head. He had answered every question, and she believed him. Everything would work out fine.

When four-thirty arrived, Hannah left to pick up Mathew, enjoying the soft warmth of the late afternoon. She stopped in front of the house to find him relaxed and waiting on the wide porch in a grey pinstriped suit.

"You look wonderful." She couldn't believe how seriously he was taking this.

He bowed low before getting into the car, and giving her the once over. "You look pretty wonderful yourself." He smiled broadly.

Hannah drove uptown to her affluent neighborhood, trying to see it through his eyes. As she pulled up in front of the house, she had to smile.

"Wow, Hannah, you live here?" he asked as if amazed.

"You have a problem with that?" she grinned, slapping him playfully on the leg.

Instead of taking him to the kitchen door, Hannah led Mathew to the front porch, wondering if he liked the white climbing roses on the trellis near the entrance, or if he thought their house too gaudy or overdone.

Charlie Collins met them at the door, and after a moment's hesitation, he took Mathew's offered hand as his daughter introduced them. Hannah's mother came up behind Charlie, peeking over his shoulder. When Mr. Collins stepped aside, she immediately took Mathew by the arm and pulled him inside.

"So you're the man my daughter's been going crazy over?" she asked. "You sure are a fine gentleman."

"Mother!" Hannah blurted.

Mathew grinned, but his smile faded when he looked at Mr. Collins. Hannah hurried to break the silence.

"Ma, Dad, this is Mathew Stephens," she said.

"Hello, Mathew," Charlie said, motioning them toward the formal dining room. "I think Hannah's mother is ready to serve dinner."

Hannah followed her father into the dining room, drawing Mathew behind her. She didn't like the disapproval in her father's eyes, but they would deal with it later. For now, she wanted everything to be perfect. The smell of fresh-baked rolls and grilled chicken added to her expectations; she had spent the afternoon kneading dough and making her favorite salad.

"You two just sit down," Deborah said pleasantly as she hurried into the kitchen. "I'll be back in a minute."

The table setting surprised Hannah. Her mother's wedding china sparkled, and an exquisite lace tablecloth covered the dark wood table. Mathew held out a chair for her and she dropped into it, smiling up at him.

After Mathew and Hannah took their seats, her father settled in his chair and immediately began questioning her suitor.

"So, Mathew, what do you do for a living?"

"I'm a judge for Crystal Springs," Mathew replied, his hands folded in his lap. Hannah tried not to giggle. He looked like a kid who had been sent to the principal's office.

"Very good," her father grumbled, as if unwilling to be impressed. "So do you really like my daughter or are you using her just so you can say you dated a black woman?"

"Daddy!" Hannah gasped, staring at her father in surprise, her cheeks heating up. How could he ask something like that?

"No, it's okay, Hannah," Mathew reassured her. His gaze met hers across the table and he nodded slightly before turning to study her father. "I am very attracted to your daughter. She's beautiful and smart and more importantly, she makes me happy."

Hannah smiled. She should have known he would say just the right thing.

Just then, Deborah brought out a big platter of chicken surrounded by grilled onions and tomatoes and placed it near the center of the table.

"What do you do for fun, Mathew?" Charlie asked, pressing on with his questions.

"Nothing important really," Mathew replied politely. "I like to fish and put down traps for wild possum and stuff like that. What do you do, sir?"

"You don't have to call me sir," her father muttered. "My name's Charlie Collins. I own a bakery downtown."

Hannah looked up as Mathew began to cough, lowering his water glass to the table with a thud.

"Are you okay, Mathew?" Mr. Collins asked, looking concerned.

"No, not really," Mathew replied, his eyes watering. "I think I might be coming down with something." He mopped his damp forehead with a linen napkin.

Mathew cleared his throat again. How the hell could he sit here eating in the home of the man whose downfall he was plotting? Looking around the table at the woman he loved and her parents who were trying to make a good impression on their daughter's boyfriend, he felt his heart constrict. Am I that evil?

"Hannah, maybe you should drive Mathew home," her mother said, her gaze sympathetic. The look in them made

Mathew feel even more ashamed, and he lowered his eyes to the table.

"He's only been here a few minutes, and we haven't eaten yet," Hannah protested. Still, she looked concerned.

He shook his head, but couldn't force any words out.

"Take your man home so he can rest, sweetie."

Hannah nodded and laid her napkin on the table, jumping up to come around the table and help Mathew to his feet. He coughed a little more as he rose, covering his mouth with his hand.

Mr. Collins rose, too, reaching over to pat Mathew on the back. "You're welcome here again, son," he said.

"Thank you," Mathew finally choked out. With another loud cough behind his hand, he cleared his throat and turned to Hannah's mother. "Mrs. Collins, thank you for inviting me."

Mrs. Collins smiled and followed them to the front door.

Hannah guided Mathew back to her car and settled him in the passenger seat. The drive home gave him a chance to get himself under control, and by the time the car pulled in his driveway, he had decided that things would work out on their own. He just had to handle the problem very carefully.

"Would you like to spend the night again?" he asked before getting out of the car.

"Not tonight," she replied, studying him. "You're certainly not up to it. I really should go home and let you get some rest."

Guilt overtook him, and Mathew felt a strong desire to tell her his feelings. "You are so understanding, Hannah. I know this relationship is very young, but I think I love you."

He saw her gaze soften, her eyes filling with tears. "Oh, Mathew, I love you, too. Come here."

He leaned back into the car, and she kissed him, intertwining her tongue with his, and Mathew knew he wanted her, body, heart and soul. With a whispered goodbye, she started the car. He moved away and with a final wave, she was gone.

Mathew went inside and closed the door. How could he be the Grand Wizard of the local KKK and in love with the very thing they opposed at the same time? When he saw Hannah, he looked beyond the surface, beyond the color of her skin. She was a beautiful, successful woman who cared... no loved him as much as he believed he loved her. He didn't need anything else.

Chapter Fifteen

Sunday morning, Danny decided to take a walk to settle his nerves. In the past, he would have gone to Frances' Lunch and Deli Shop. Now that he knew the owner was involved in the KKK, he wouldn't go near the place. Instead, he walked up the block and back, arriving home to the smell of bacon and coffee.

"It's a shame we have to miss church because the Reverend is in the KKK," Connie said. "I would never have believed it."

"After tonight, everything will return to normal," Danny reassured her. "And we'll be able to go to church again."

"What will the church do if the Reverend is in jail?" Her large brown eyes were filled with worry and doubt.

Unfortunately, he didn't have any answers for her. He couldn't change what would happen this evening, and he couldn't make Reverend Butler become a decent human being in time to keep him from going to jail. The thought of a minister committing murder and breaking God's laws while acting like a high and mighty holy man to his parishioners made him angry.

"Connie, you're always worried about something," he answered without thinking. He turned and walked out of the kitchen, resisting the urge to punch the wall.

What the hell were they going to do when all this hit the fan?

* * *

Geoff couldn't wait until evening. Adrenaline coursed through him, and he was excited about finally being able to put the Klansmen behind bars. They had gotten away with murder for far too long. He smiled at his reflection in the bathroom mirror, and decided to shave. The tantalizing aroma of blueberry pancakes cooking on the griddle downstairs, wafted up to him, and he hurried to the kitchen, eyeing the huge stack and a plate of sausage links on the table.

"What's all this?" he asked, moving up behind his wife at the stove.

"Pancakes and sausage links," Rosie said, snuggling against him as he slid his arms around her. "I decided to make your favorite breakfast. This is a big day for you, and you're going to need lots of energy."

"You're the best, sweetheart." Geoff kissed her smooth cheek and released her, sitting down at the small breakfast table.

"What time do you have to be at the station tonight?" she asked, looking over her shoulder.

"Seven o'clock sharp," he told her, expertly spearing three big flapjacks from the steaming stack in front of him. After adding four sausages to his plate, he reached for the butter.

Connie brought over the remaining pancakes she had cooked and sat down opposite him, but she made no move to fill her own plate. "I hope everything goes smoothly, tonight."

"Me, too," he said quietly.

Rosie looked across the table at him, her eyes wide and glistening with the sheen of unshed tears. "Geoff, be careful, okay?" she pleaded, reaching across the table for his hand. "When you come home tonight, I'll make it worth your while."

Geoff squeezed her hand gently, trying to lighten the somber mood. "How?" he asked teasingly, wriggling his eyebrows in a suggestive leer.

She giggled and brushed the back of her hand across her eyes before smiling and filling her plate. "I'll give you a back and neck rub," she offered. When he said nothing, her smile deepened. "And any other kind of rub you want," she promised.

Geoff remembered her promise on his way to work that evening. He hoped everything went as planned, and that no one got hurt, but he knew that in this type of situation, there was always the potential for something to go terribly wrong.

At seven o'clock, Chief Waldron, Geoff, and the twenty-five officers scheduled for the operation were seated in the precinct's conference room. The Chief approached the podium, his white hair neatly slicked back. Everyone knew he had prepared this speech to pump them up.

"Okay, listen up. We've had a change in plans," he said. "At eight-thirty sharp, we'll set up a perimeter around Reverend Butler's home, not Judge Stephen's. This is the big one, boys. We don't want anyone getting hurt, so there's absolutely no room for error." He surveyed the assembled group. "Keep your positions. No shooting unless it's necessary. I want to take these bastards alive. Any questions?"

No one said a word.

Waldron nodded and stepped down from the podium, moving over to stand behind Geoff. "I think we're ready," he commented, watching the men disperse to don their gear and pick up their assigned weapons. "I hope Danny is okay."

"Danny knows what he's doing, Chief," Geoff answered with a shrug, even though he, too, was worried. "I'm sure he'll be fine. If everything goes according to plan, no one should get hurt, and we'll all be heroes."

His face solemn, Chief Waldron nodded. "I hope you're right."

Danny and several Klan members sat in Reverend Butler's personal library, waiting for Mathew. The room was filled with blond oak furniture and was nowhere near as grand as the Judge's home. With each passing moment, Danny felt his nerves stretch and grow taut like a bowstring that had been tightened too much. If Stephens didn't arrive soon, the biggest fish would escape the net the police were carefully setting up outside. His next thought shook him. If the judge showed up now, he would see the trap being laid. Stephens could drive away and notify his fellow Klan members by phone, ruining everything.

"In the meantime," Reverend Butler continued from the front of the room, "Danny Pummel has been found worthy to become a conditional member of this Klan until he passes his initiation. Danny, do you have your dues?"

"Yes, sir, I do," Danny replied, snapping out of his misgivings and handing Reverend Butler the required amount. He briefly wondered if he would ever get the money back. If he hadn't been so worried about what was happening outside, he might have smiled at the thought.

"Maybe I should phone Judge Stephens," Reverend Butler suggested after a long moment of silence.

"Yeah, I think that would be a good idea," another member agreed. There were murmurs of assent throughout the room.

Almost as soon as the words left his mouth, the phone rang, making Danny tense as he wondered if all hell was about to break loose.

Reverend Butler punched the button for the speakerphone. "Hello?"

"Reverend, this is Mathew." The judge's voice sounded weak.

"Mathew, we were just wondering about you." Reverend Butler leaned toward the phone. "We can't finish planning until you get here."

"I'm not going to make it, sorry. I'm so sick, I can barely walk," Mathew said.

Danny and the others heard the sound of coughing through the speaker.

"What are we going to do about Wednesday's ride out?" the Reverend asked, looking around at the other men in the room. Danny followed his glance and saw several heads eagerly nodding.

"Might have to call it off," a cough cut off Mathew's words. After a pause, he went on, "I don't think it's a good idea to talk about it over the phone."

"I agree, Mathew," the Reverend agreed, holding up his hand to still the murmuring in the group before him. "I hope you feel better. I'll call tomorrow and let you know how the meeting went."

Danny inwardly sighed with relief as the Reverend hung up and looked around the room again. "It seems we'll have to postpone our plans, but you will still leave here with the word of the Lord, our God. Tonight I want to talk about affirmative action and the meaning of racism."

Several men clapped. The Reverend accepted the encouragement and went on.

"Affirmative action is discrimination against the white man here in America. The government is discriminating against us by telling us who to hire in our companies. We shouldn't be expected to hire a man just because he's black. It's not right to make white folks hire minorities, especially when we all know they are mediocre workers at best."

The men nodded and murmured in agreement.

Reverend Baker continued. "What is racism? In America today, you are considered a *racist* if you don't want to be around poverty-stricken minorities. You are a *racist* if you want to live separately with others of your own kind. The Bible says, and I quote, 'Be separate.' In my book, there is really no such thing as racism. It comes down to choices, and I choose not to associate with people who belong to an inferior race."

"Just because we want separate clubs and societies, we are *considered* racist," the Reverend continued. "Why that's ludicrous. Are we being racist when we don't permit women to join a gentlemen's club?"

The men in the room answered in unison. "No!"

"Are we being racist when we keep boys and girls separate in the Boy Scouts and Girl Scouts?"

"No!"

"Well, this isn't any different. We have the right to choose our associates. It says so in the Constitution of the United States!"

"Yeah!"

"This is the Devil's plan to destroy God's will. God says to be separate. I want to end my message by saying, go out and be separate. Mix not with the world. Look at Sodom and Gomorrah, a perfect example of what such wrongs can create."

Applause thundered through the room, and several men shouted "Amen," until the Reverend bowed and seated himself to continue with the rest of the meeting.

By now the police, wearing bulletproof vests and carrying enough firepower to equip a small army, had surrounded Reverend Butler's home. He wished he could warn them that the Klan's boss had called off sick, but it was too late. They would have to be satisfied with capturing the majority of Klansmen and hope they could either arrest their leader later or get one of the others to rat out the judge. A loud birdcall sounded, and pandemonium ensued.

The front door crashed open, and officers burst into the home. Danny heard them coming toward the room where he sat. The men around him also heard the commotion and reached for their weapons. As police officers invaded the library, Danny jumped from his seat and pulled out his own weapon, pointing it at the rest of the Klan members.

"Freeze! Put your hands in the air where we can see them!" Danny looked around at the men he had applauded with moments earlier. They had trusted him, allowed him among them, accepting him for his skin color without knowing his true beliefs.

Several of the men, including Reverend Butler, looked at Danny with hard, angry eyes. Others showed shock that one of their own had betrayed them. Many hands raised in the air, but Luke Fields reached into his pocket, pulled out a nine-millimeter Glock, and shot Danny three times.

Surprised, Danny felt pain blossom in his chest and side, and his head felt like someone had hit it with a sledgehammer. He looked down to see a bullet lodged just above his heart in the Kevlar protection. Putting his hand to the pain in his side, he came up with blood, lots of it, running between his fingers to drip to the floor. Danny's world started spinning as he pointed his own gun at Luke, but he couldn't focus well enough to take the shot.

One of the officers, coming through the door, shot Luke Fields in the chest. A red splotch appeared on the man's shirt, and he slumped to the floor, eyes wide and accusing as he stared at Danny in disbelief.

"Everyone, up against the wall and spread your legs! Now!" another officer yelled.

The Klansmen quickly did as they were told, propping their hands against the wall as more police officers filed into the room. Several officers read them their rights, while removing the men's guns and handcuffing them one by one. Geoff and the Chief burst through the door and watched in horror as Danny lifted his bloody hand and collapsed.

"Call an ambulance, now!" Geoff yelled. He knelt next to Danny and applied pressure to his wounds. Danny reached for him, but he couldn't seem to make his muscles work.

"Danny, stay with me, buddy," Geoff said. "Hang in there."

Danny smiled through his pain. "Glad you could make it."

Geoff returned his grin. "I wouldn't have missed it for the world."

"Thanks," Danny muttered, breathing in short pants as pain gripped him harder. He didn't feel the blood running down his face from the wound in his temple. "Guess I should have continued pretending to be one of them and allowed you to arrest me instead of playing the hero."

"Just hang on, buddy," Geoff said, looking down at him. "The ambulance is on the way."

Danny reached up to grasp Geoff's sleeve. "If I don't make it... tell Connie... tell Connie I'm... sorry," he whispered through ragged breaths. His chest ached from the bullet's impact against his vest, and the warmth pooling beneath him could only mean one thing.

Geoff shook his head. "You tell her, man. I am not going to piss that woman off." He stretched his lips into a semblance of a grin. "You're going to be all right, Danny. Just hold on."

Darkness nibbled at Danny's consciousness, and he tried to see what was happening around him. Chief Waldron stood in the doorway, speaking into his cell phone and watching as officers escorted the prisoners to the various squad cars. They had missed Mathew Stephens, and Danny knew that mistake could bite them in the ass later. But for now, he didn't really care. As soon as the thought crossed his mind, he heard a siren wailing in the distance, coming closer, but he couldn't hold on any longer. Closing his eyes, he allowed the blackness take him.

Geoff followed the ambulance to the hospital, calling Rosie and Connie and asking them to meet him there with as brief an explanation as possible.

When the ambulance arrived at the Queen of Mercy Hospital, the emergency room doctor barked orders to nurses and interns over the chaos. After an initial examination, he spoke to Geoff.

"Once he's stabilized, we'll take him to the operating room. He's lost a lot of blood. I'll come out and speak with the family as soon as I know something."

Geoff nodded. Ten minutes later, he watched apprehensively as the doctor rushed after the team taking Danny to the surgical floor. The Lieutenant returned to the waiting room just as Rosie and Connie hurried in through the emergency room entrance. He was glad Rosie was here. She knew Connie well enough that she could provide support to the other woman while Danny was in surgery.

He reached out and pulled Danny's wife to him. "I'm sorry," he said, his eyes catching Rosie's over Connie's head.

"Oh, Geoff, I tried to stop him."

"I know Connie, but it was something he felt he had to do."

"And now he's going to die because of it," she sobbed.

"Connie," Rosie said, putting her arms around the other woman, "he's not going to die." She cast an imploring look at her husband.

"They just took him to surgery," he said. "He got here pretty quickly, so his chances should be good."

In his heart, he knew his words were nothing more than empty promises. No matter how good the body armor was, there was always a chance a bullet might get through. Geoff had to get back to the station, fill out his report, and help process the prisoners, but he wanted to make sure Connie had someone to stay with her. He escorted the two women to the surgical waiting room on the second floor. After checking to see if they wanted anything to drink, he left, hurrying back to the station to process the prisoners and any evidence that would keep these men behind bars. Several officers were still at the Reverend's home, searching for incriminating evidence. In the morning, they would get warrants to search the rest of the Klan's homes and businesses.

"Well, Chief, what do you think?" he asked.

"I think we screwed up." Chief Waldron looked up from the papers on his desk, his brows knitted in a frown.

"Why?" Geoff asked.

"Because we missed the main man," the Chief growled, slapping his hand on the wooden desk. "The grand pooh bah!"

Geoff nodded. "Mathew Stephens."

"When I asked Reverend Baker about him, he played dumb. He said that Stephens didn't belong to their little group and as far as he knew, the judge was home sick with the flu or something."

Geoff could tell that Chief Waldron wasn't buying it. For that matter, he didn't believe it himself.

"If that isn't the dumbest lie I've ever heard. Problem is, unless one of the Klan rats him out, we have no proof that the judge is a member. And they'll probably keep their mouths shut, figuring the Judge might be able to help them as long as he isn't behind bars."

"We can still nail him if Danny testifies otherwise. By the way, how is Danny?"

Geoff shook his head glumly. "Not good. He took a bullet to the side and was nicked in the head." He pointed to his right temple. "To be honest, Chief, it will be a miracle if Danny survives. And you know how the court views the testimony of a dead man. It'll be considered hearsay. What are we going to tell the newspapers?"

"For now, we'll just list the members we arrested," the Chief replied. "Until we find some hard evidence against Stephens or one of his Klansmen snitches on him, our hands are tied." He sighed heavily.

Gray Love

The Chief stood up and placed his arm around Geoff's slumped shoulders. "Why don't you go back to the hospital? I know you're worried. We can handle things here. I'd rather have you fresh for the morning when we start executing all those search warrants that Judge Abernathy is preparing for us."

"Thanks, Chief. I'll keep you posted."

Chapter Sixteen

Geoff found Connie and Rosie seated on a dark green sofa in the surgical waiting room. Rosie looked up and gave him a weak smile as he walked toward them. He could tell she had been crying. Her mascara ran in long black streaks down her tear-stained cheeks.

Connie looked almost comatose, her eyes glazed as if she had already cried every tear she was capable of producing. Geoff sat next to Connie and looked across the top of her head at his wife, giving her a reassuring smile.

"Any word yet?"

Rosie shook her head no.

Two hours and four cups of coffee later, the surgeon entered the waiting room, pushing a light blue surgical cap from his curly gray hair. He approached the volunteer at the check-in desk.

"Is the family of Danny Pummel here?" the doctor asked. He had a kind face, and Geoff sighed with relief. At least the doctor wasn't frowning.

The volunteer pointed to Connie, Rosie, and Geoff, and as the doctor approached, Connie jumped up off the couch, with Rosie close behind.

"I'm Danny's wife," Connie said anxiously.

The doctor came forward and extended a hand, which she nervously accepted.

"I'm Dr. Salvo, your husband's surgeon. The bullet in his side tore up his left kidney pretty bad, and I had to remove it. He lost a lot of blood and remains in critical condition. Once he leaves the recovery room, he will be transferred to intensive

Gray Love

care. If you know anyone willing to donate blood, it will offset the cost for the blood he received."

"I'll take care of that," Geoff interjected. "His fellow officers will donate whatever you need."

"Thank you," the doctor said.

"May I see him?" Connie asked, her eyes darting past the doctor to the corridor beyond. Rosie placed an arm around her friend's shoulders, and Geoff watched helplessly, uncertain what else he could do for his friend's wife.

"Please?" Connie sounded more urgent now.

"There is one other thing, Mrs. Pummel. Your husband also suffered a gunshot wound to the head and is in a coma. The neurologist is going over the CAT scans to determine if the bullet can be safely removed."

Connie cringed, and Rosie hugged her tighter. "What does that mean?"

"We don't know yet," the doctor replied. "Whether or not the bullet is removed depends on how deep it went and what part of the brain it's in. If his brain swells, the neurosurgeon will have to open his skull to relieve the pressure."

"Please, can I see him now?" Connie sobbed.

"As soon as he leaves recovery and is transferred to ICU, I'll have someone come and get you."

"Thank you, doctor," Connie said.

Two hours later, the volunteer received a phone call that Danny was in ICU.

"The family of Danny Pummel," she called out.

Connie, Geoff, and Rosie hurried to the desk.

"Mrs. Pummel? Your husband is out of recovery and has been taken to ICU. Do you know where that's at?"

Connie shook her head no.

The nurse gave her directions. "One of you can come with her for now, but you'll only be able to stay fifteen minutes. The nurse can give you a schedule for visiting hours."

Rosie looked at Geoff questioningly, and he nodded. "You go ahead, honey. You'll be more helpful to Connie than I will. I'll wait here for you."

He watched them hurry away; Connie almost sagging as she clung to Rosie as though her life depended on it. Walking over to the coffee machine in the waiting room, he cursed himself for allowing Danny to go into that meeting alone.

You couldn't have done anything, his rational mind told him. *Yeah, but I shouldn't have let him do this in the first place*, he argued back, even though he knew that without his friend's undercover work, they would never have found enough evidence to arrest the Klan. Danny would not have listened anyway.

After meeting the ICU nurse in charge of her husband, Connie stood over the bed in his private room and watched his still figure. Blood and saline solution dripped through IVs attached to his arms, while other machines kept track of his blood pressure, heart rate, and oxygen level. She reached for his hand.

"Damn it, Danny," she whispered accusingly. "You promised you wouldn't get hurt. You promised!"

He didn't move, and she felt Rosie's steadying presence beside her. Connie turned to her. "There's something I should have told him before he left tonight, something important." Connie burst into tears.

"What is it, Connie?" Rosie fought back her own tears. "Just tell him now. They say that when a person is in a coma, he can still hear you. Tell him now."

Connie turned back to Danny. "I missed my period this month," she said, looking down at him, and wishing he would open his eyes. "So I got a pregnancy test at the drugstore."

"And?" Rosie urged, squeezing her hand.

"You have to be okay, Danny," Connie said, "because... because you're going to be a daddy."

"Oh, Connie," Rosie said, pulling Connie into a comforting embrace. "That's wonderful news. I know that somehow, Danny heard you, and he's very happy."

"We've been trying for over a year," Connie sobbed. "Now it's happened, and he might not make it. He may never see or hold his child."

"Don't talk that way," Rosie said. "He's going to make it. You have to believe that."

"It's so hard, not knowing. What if he never comes out of the coma? What if his brain is damaged and he ends up a vegetable? That happens, you know?"

"I know, sweetie, but no matter what, you'll always have a part of him with you. Just remember that."

* * *

Early Monday morning, Hannah went downstairs to breakfast and found her parents sitting at the kitchen table, intently reading the morning paper.

A sense of foreboding swept through her. "Mom? Dad? What's wrong?"

"Nothing's wrong." Her father pushed the newspaper toward her.

She looked down at the headlines on the front page and read, "Suspected Klan members behind bars."

She held her hand over her heart as she read the list of names: Reverend Butler, Dr. James Corley, Dean and Sky Frances, Howard Young, Robert Hemming, Bobby Robichaux, and Chris Thibodaux. Earlier in the week, Ken Lewis had been arrested and charged with first degree murder in the shooting death of Taylor Henderson. Luke Fields had been shot and killed, and Detective Danny Pummel was in critical condition at the hospital. She scanned the rest of the article. Thank God, there was no mention of Mathew. She sighed with relief.

"I just can't believe it." Her mother used a napkin to dab at the corners of her eyes. "We know these men, conduct business, and attend services with them. How can they be guilty of such horrendous things?" She glanced up at Hannah, a questioning look on her face.

"I don't know, Ma," Hannah said, her chest tight with emotion. "At least we won't have to worry about them harassing us. I have to run an errand before I go to work this morning, so I'm heading out."

She planted a kiss on her mother's cheek, hugged her father, and went out to her car.

She had to talk to Mathew. Even though he had denied being in the Klan, and his name wasn't in the paper, her instincts told her that something wasn't right.

Chapter Seventeen

Hannah drove straight to Mathew's house, her mind a jumble of hope and fear. Even though his name had not been listed with the others, it didn't bolster her confidence. Maybe it was nothing, or maybe her woman's intuition was coming on too strong. Was it possible she was so much in love with this man that she couldn't see past the surface? What did she really know about him?

She thought back to the many conversations they'd had – she had shared so much, and he so little. Every time Hannah asked a personal question, he dismissed or evaded it. No matter how hard she tried, either teasingly or directly, he shut down whenever she brought up the subject of his personal life.

She pulled into the driveway of his large home and sat there, taking a quiet moment to reflect as she surveyed his property – a plantation run by a white master, with heaven only knows how many Negro slaves. Across the fields rippling with grain, she spotted two of the hired hands, their backs bent as they struggled with a piece of machinery. At least they had modern equipment to use.

The front door opened, and Mathew stepped onto the wide veranda. As he reached down to pick up the morning paper, he spotted her car.

"Hannah?" he called.

She opened the car door and swung her long legs out of the vehicle. As she stood up, he waved, a huge smile lighting his features as he hurried down the steps.

"Hey, what are you doing here so early on a Monday morning," he asked, circling her waist with his large hands and sweeping her off her feet.

She looked at him, unsure of what to say. Wasn't this what she wanted? If she ignored what she felt, could she simply lose herself in this man's charm and never worry about whatever secrets he might be hiding? Deep down inside, Hannah knew that wasn't her way.

His smile dimming, he set her down and leaned back to look at her, a questioning look in his eyes.

"Okay, what's wrong?" he asked. "Surely it can't be all that bad, can it?"

"I need to talk to you about something that deeply troubles me," she said. "Can we go inside?"

"Sure." He looked perplexed as he led her into the house and down the hallway to the kitchen.

The aroma of freshly made coffee called to her, and, for a second, she lost herself in the tranquility of it before mentally kicking herself. No matter how much his answers might upset her; she had to know the truth.

"Would you like some coffee? I just made it," he offered.

"No, thanks, please sit down and take a look at the newspaper." She crossed her arms and waited.

Shooting another questioning look at her, he sat and pulled the paper out of its plastic wrapper. When he opened it, she saw a quick flash of horror and recognition sweep across his face.

"Oh, my God," he said quietly. He looked up at her with a sick expression on his face.

"It's true, isn't it?" she said. "Those men are alleged Klan members, and I saw by the expression on your face that you know them. They are the men in that picture upstairs. Am I right? Don't lie to me."

She could tell he was stunned by both the newspaper's headlines and her direct approach, but she had to know for certain. In a way, this was a test. Would he tell her the truth, or would he simply deny everything? She had no proof; all she had was a few offbeat statements he had made regarding blacks and her heart, telling her that this man, her beloved, was not all that he seemed.

He got up, moving to stand before her. "Yes, my love, I know these men. More than that, I'm one of these men."

She shuddered, her mind held in a tight blanket of numbing pain. "Why did you lie to me, Mathew? Why?" Her voice trembled as tears slid down her cheeks.

He tried to take her icy hands in his, but she snatched them away as if he had branded her.

"How could you be part of this... this lynch mob? How could I allow you lead me down the rosy path of so-called love while all along you were hiding this horrible truth from me?" Tears overwhelmed her with a violence that shook her entire body

"Hannah, please..." he tried again.

"Please what?" She lowered her voice, but the words came out harsh and angry. "Please let you make a fool of me? Please let you kill my family? I know that the Klan was planning on hitting my family next. What else could you possibly want from me?"

He didn't try to touch her again. He just stood there, close enough for her to touch, and she hoped he would move. Because what she really wanted was to rip out his heart, wrap it in her pain, and hand it back to him on one of his expensive china platters. Instead, she bunched her hands into fists and screamed a long primal wail of agony.

Still, he did not move as she vented her anger. After several moments, she finally stopped, exhausted by the emotional weight of his betrayal. Then he took her in his arms, pulling her close as he smoothed the flowing locks away from her tear-stained face.

"How could you? How could you?" she whispered, knowing in her heart that there was nothing he could say that would justify his actions, at least, none that would relieve the unbearable ache in her soul.

Finally, he spoke. "Hannah, I have no excuse for lying to you. I am so much in love with you that I allowed my emotions to smother my good sense." He had the grace to look away from her searching gaze.

"How can you say that you love me?" she said, her voice growing stronger. "How can love exist in a world of lies and hatred? Did you think I would never find out? Did you think I was too stupid to see inside to the person you really are?" She paused to take a breath. "What kind of relationship did you think we could possibly have? Did you honestly believe I would never know you were one of those cowards hiding beneath the white hoods and robes of the Klan? Or that your fellow Klansmen would allow such a relationship to exist?"

"I... I don't know what I thought," he replied, miserably.

She struggled out of his arms and moved away, turning her back. "I guess you thought I was nothing more than a black bimbo who couldn't see through the fog of sex I believed was love."

She hurried from the kitchen and out the door, his protests lingering in the air behind her. Jumping into her car, she threw it in reverse, and shot out of the driveway. A loud honk and screeching brakes got her attention, and she gasped as a UPS truck skidded out of control behind her. Shifting the car into drive, she jammed the gas pedal to the floorboard and got out of the way of the vehicle bearing down on her.

Scanning the road in front of her for traffic, she also kept an eye on the truck, which came to a lumbering halt against Mathew's fence. Keeping the gas pedal floored, Hannah sped away from the man she had thought she loved more than any other. A man who had made her heart flutter with joy. How could she have been so blind?

Chapter Eighteen

Geoff Tray walked into the police station early Monday morning and headed for the Chief's office. He found Waldron sitting at his desk, going through some files.

"Any news about Danny?" the Chief asked.

"Nothing's changed," Geoff replied. "Rosie stayed at the hospital with Connie last night, but she called this morning and said he is still in a coma. Damn, I shouldn't have allowed him to talk me into this."

"Well, you can take half that load of guilt and lay it right here," the Chief said. "But that's not the only problem we have." He sighed in frustration.

"What's that? Oh, no, don't tell me. You had to release them."

The phone rang. It was the administrative officer.

"No. No comment," the Chief said vehemently before slamming down the phone. "I swear if one more reporter calls… You'd think they would know better, especially on a Monday. I hate Mondays."

"What happened?"

"Some big shot with a lot of pull happened, that's what," the Chief said. "There isn't enough solid evidence to hold these guys, not when you have a bunch of high-powered legal hounds whispering in the judge's ear. The only one we were able to retain was Ken Lewis, and that's only because the judge denied bail. Unless Danny recovers…"

Geoff jumped up from his chair and started pacing. "Unless? He's going to recover, Chief. He has to."

Gray Love

Waldron picked up the newspaper and tossed it in front of Geoff. "Look on the bright side. Everyone knows who they are, even if they never come to trial. Their secret is out. Hiding under their white hoods won't protect them any longer."

* * *

Connie sat in her husband's hospital room, her cold hands enclosing one of his. She watched the slow rise and fall of his chest, feeling each breath as it moved in and out of his lungs. Danny's eyes were closed, and he looked more at peace than he had in weeks. She once had heard someone say that whenever a person goes in a coma, they were usually making plans for their future life. She hoped that, if Danny didn't make it, his future plans included her. As that thought hit home, a tear escaped her reddened eyes and slid down her cheek. She wiped it away angrily, wondering where it could have come from. She had shed so many tears since learning about the shooting that she found it hard to believe there were any left.

Rosie walked into the room. She had gone home to freshen up, and looked less harried than she had earlier. "Hi, honey," she said. "It's your turn now."

Connie gave her a questioning look.

"You need to get away for a little bit," Rosie said. "Run home, get some clean clothes, take a quick shower, and freshen up a bit. I'll stay here until you get back."

"I can't leave him," Connie said, looking at the still figure on the bed.

"You can, and you must," Rosie said. "You have to take care of yourself." When Connie looked like she would refuse again, she added, "You have to think about the life inside you. If you don't take proper care of yourself, the baby will suffer."

Connie slowly got to her feet, her hands still lingering on her husband's.

"I know you're right, Rosie, but what if something happens while I'm gone?"

"It will happen whether you're here or not," Rosie replied reasonably. "Besides, you're leaving him in good hands." She smiled encouragingly at her friend.

"Okay, I'll be back soon." Connie turned and left. Although her body left the hospital, her heart remained in that room with her husband.

Chapter Nineteen

A month later, Hannah sat at her desk with the office door closed, working on case files to keep her mind off Mathew. She had read the first paragraph of the open file in front of her at least ten times, but she had no idea what it said.

The office phone rang, jarring her from her thoughts. Without thinking, she answered.

"Hi, Hannah," Mathew said softly.

Hannah exhaled sharply. "Why are you calling?"

"Hannah, just listen," he pleaded, his voice laced with misery.

Before he could say another word, she slammed the phone down, her heart tight in her chest. She wouldn't listen to him try and explain the lies or the devastation he had left behind. She had trusted him once, but she would never make that mistake again. She couldn't believe the things he had done, couldn't accept the casual cruelty of his actions against people of her race.

Her stomach roiled, and she took several deep breaths to keep from throwing up. Every time she thought about him, she felt queasy. But as Hannah thought about her bouts of nausea, she realized it had been happening a lot. In the month since she had learned the truth about Mathew, Hannah had lost weight, wasn't sleeping well, and couldn't look at or stand the smell of certain foods she used to love without wanting to vomit. The thought brought another, more troubling possibility to mind, and she made a note to stop at the drugstore on the way home.

Ten minutes later, her cell phone rang. After hesitating a moment, she answered it.

"Hi, Hannah, it's Kenneth."

Hannah shook her head. She had never contacted him to apologize, but still he called her. He was definitely a good man.

"How are you doing?" he asked.

"I'm working." She hoped she didn't sound as depressed as she felt.

"Last time we were supposed to go on a date, you were sick. You never called me back," he said cheerfully. "I've been worried about you."

She hastened to reassure him "I'm fine, really. It's just that I have had a particularly heavy case load this past month."

After a short pause, he added, "I was wondering if you would like to go out tomorrow. I'm back in town early, and I have some good news."

Hannah ignored her initial reaction to dismiss him; she needed to have some fun, and Kenneth truly did care about her. "I'd love to."

"Great," he announced. "I'll pick you up at seven, okay?"

"Sounds good to me," Hannah replied numbly. She punched the "off" button on the phone, set it on the desk, and leaned back in her chair, trying to easy some of the tiredness from her body.

For the first time in a month, she had a date. It was past time; it did her no good to hope that Mathew would ever be on her social agenda again. Even if she wanted to take him back, too many barriers stood between them. Although her parents had never said anything about Mathew's sudden disappearance from her life, she knew they wondered and worried about what had happened, especially since her and Mathew's relationship had been on the fast track.

She leaned forward, resting her forehead on her arms. *Why can't I fall in love with a nice man like Kenneth? Someone who* would give me the moon if I asked, or call me all day long just to say he loved me? What's wrong with me?

She went back to work, but accomplished little the rest of the day. Finally, she drove home, forgetting to stop at the drugstore, and picked at her dinner before falling into bed early, trying to hide from the pain in her heart.

* * *

Connie Pummel's doorbell rang shortly before 10 p.m. She put aside the book she was reading and went to the door. Flipping on the porch light, she peered through the hole in the door and then quickly opened it.

"Geoff, Rosie, what are you doing here at this hour?"

Rosie reached out and pulled Connie into a hug.

"It's Danny," Geoff said quietly. "You need to come with us."

"No, no – he's not dead. He's not dead… is he?" Connie's face was completely drained of color.

"We need you to come to the hospital with us, now," Rosie said, reaching around Connie to collect the other woman's purse from the hall table.

Connie sagged against Geoff. He helped her into the back seat of his unmarked police car next to Rosie, then ran around and jumped in, hitting the lights and siren.

They arrived at the hospital in record time. Geoff hurried the ladies into the elevator. When they reached the third floor, the doors opened and Connie ran toward Danny's room. The doctor met her at the door.

"I'm sorry, Mrs. Pummel," he said.

She sped to Danny's bedside. He was very still, and his face was calm and peaceful. Connie leaned down and took one of his cold hands in hers; her mind refusing to accept what she suspected was true as her eyes subconsciously flew to the instruments next to the bed. The readings were the same as they had been earlier in the day.

"Mrs. Pummel? Mrs. Pummel, please."

The doctor had entered the room and was speaking to her. She looked at him through eyes filled with pain.

"Mrs. Pummel, I'm sorry. Your husband is brain-dead. I need your permission to take him off life support."

"No," she said quietly, "you can't. It will kill him."

"Connie," Geoff said, coming up behind her. "Danny's gone. The doctor said there is no more brain activity. You have to let him go in peace."

Rosie joined Geoff at Connie's side, hugging her friend, tears streaming down her cheeks.

"I can't," Connie told them. "I can't. I didn't get to say goodbye. I have to say goodbye, Geoff." She turned to look at Geoff and pleaded. "Can't we just leave everything on until I tell him goodbye?"

Geoff looked over at the doctor and received a nod.

"Sure, honey, it's okay. Do you want us to stay with you?"

"No, it's okay." She smiled up at him bleakly. "I'll be fine."

"Of course, you will," Rosie said. "You have to think about the little one inside you. That's what Danny would want you to do, and he would want you to take care of yourself."

Geoff placed a beefy hand on her shoulder. "We'll be right outside if you need us."

Connie nodded. Then she turned back to her husband, leaning down to whisper, "Danny, I know you have to go. It's the best thing for you. I'll take care of our baby for both of us. I wish I could tell you whether or not it's a boy or a girl, but the doctor said they can't determine that until I am eighteen to twenty weeks pregnant. But I promise you this, my love. As our baby grows, I'll tell him or her all about you and what a wonderful father you would have been. Be happy where you are, and one day, we'll both be with you."

She laid her head on his chest and wondered about the barely beating heart within, so unlike the strong thumping she had grown accustomed to over the past three years of marriage. Touching his face one last time, she turned to the doctor, who had retreated to a far corner of the room to give her a little privacy.

"Please disconnect everything so I can see him as he used to be," she said.

The doctor nodded to two nurses, waiting in the hallway. They came in and removed the tubes, needles, and oxygen that were no longer necessary. When they finished, they pushed the equipment to the back of the room and left.

Connie leaned over and kissed her husband for the last time as his heart slowed and came to a complete halt. Her tears dropped onto his still face, and she took a tissue from the bedside table and wiped them off. Turning, she left the room without looking back.

"I really don't want to be alone in that house another night," she told them.

Geoff and Rosie took Connie home and helped her pack a suitcase with some clothing and things she would need, before taking her to their house. Rosie stayed with her in the spare bedroom until Connie cried herself into a deep sleep. She walked back into the living room where Geoff sat staring at the silent TV.

"Connie's sleeping, dear. I'm going to stay with her, in case she wakes during the night and needs something, okay?"

Geoff nodded. "You go on, sweetheart. I think I'll sit here awhile longer."

"Should we call the Chief?" she asked.

"Not tonight," he told her. "No sense in waking him. It can wait until morning."

The next morning, Geoff called Chief Waldron and told him about Danny.

"I'm so sorry, Geoff," the Chief said. "How's Connie?"

"Not good," Geoff told him. "We'll keep her here with us, accompany her while she makes the arrangements, and help her get through the funeral. I don't think there's anything more we can do for now."

"Okay, Geoff, I'll put you on paid leave until everything is sorted out. You take care, son."

Chapter Twenty

Hannah decided to take a relaxing bath before her date with Kenneth. Even so, as she climbed the stairs, she was betrayed by thoughts of Mathew Stephens and his hungry kisses.

An hour later, Hannah sat at her vanity, putting on make-up. Kenneth would be there any moment. Hannah applied a light application of powder to her face and brushed her hair one last time. When Kenneth arrived, she greeted him at the front door, where he produced two dozen red roses.

"These are for you," he said, bowing slightly.

She smiled. "Thank you, Kenneth. You're so sweet."

"I like the dress," he said with approval, his gaze roaming over her body from head to toe and back again. "Very nice."

Hannah looked down at the body-hugging white dress she had chosen, accented with simple silver jewelry and white sandals. She knew the outfit looked good, but his frank appraisal brought a rosy color to her cheeks.

"Why, thank you, kind sir," she responded, dropping into a small curtsey.

He laughed out loud, reaching for her arm. "Let's go eat."

"Let me put these in a vase first, and I'll be right with you."

As she took the flowers into the kitchen, she ran into her mother.

"How beautiful! Are they from Kenneth?" her mother asked.

"Yes, ma, they are. Would you mind putting them in a vase for me?"

"I'll take care of them. You just enjoy your date," her mother said as she took the flowers and laid them on the counter top to go in search of a large enough vase.

Kenneth took her to Dominique's, a five-star restaurant downtown. He pressed a bill into the maitre d's hand, and the host seated them at a private booth near a window overlooking City View Lake.

Hannah surveyed the gorgeous view of the lighted city beyond their window as they waited for their waiter to bring the menus.

"This is wonderful. You didn't have to."

"A pretty lady deserves only the best," he said with a smile. "And you definitely qualify."

Hannah knew Kenneth wanted her with every searching glance he gave her, but she couldn't imagine anything closer than friendship between them. Still, she said, "That's very flattering."

"Believe me, it's not flattery, just plain and simple truth." He paused a moment, as if waiting for her to say something, and then leaned forward. "I have something to tell you, Hannah."

"You sound so serious," she said quietly, her hands clenching in her lap. "What is it?"

"When I was out of town, a producer from a record company heard me play. He offered me a $200,000 bonus to sign a contract with them."

"That's wonderful!" Genuine excitement filled her voice.

He reached across the table, and after a moment of hesitation, she placed her hand in his.

"I'm in love with you, Hannah."

"Please," Hannah stammered, heat crawling up her neck as she pulled her hand back. "Even though you've asked me out many times, we've never even dated. You really don't know a thing about me."

The waiter came to take their order, interrupting the uncomfortable conversation.

Kenneth ordered the best wine in the restaurant, and she wondered if that was his way of proving his love for her. They both ordered steak with steamed vegetables. When the waiter left, Kenneth asked about her day, and the talk became more comfortable.

The wine came, and he made a big show of swirling and sniffing it, as if trying to impress her with his savoir faire. They sipped wine and enjoyed each other's company while eating dinner.

Afterward, Kenneth drove a few blocks to City View Lake, bringing back memories of her time with Mathew at his private lake. She pushed the thought away as he parked on the bank overlooking the glittering water and turned to gaze at Hannah with admiration. He lifted a hand and stroked her long hair.

"I want you."

Hannah pulled away from his touch. "What are you doing?"

He reached for her again, a pained look on his face when she pressed further into the seat. "What's wrong? Why won't you let me touch you?"

Unshed tears brimmed at the corner of her eyes. She had hurt him, this man who had done nothing wrong and treated her with respect. "It isn't you. I just have a lot on my mind."

"Like what? You can tell me."

Silent moments passed as her mind tried to find the right words to express her feelings without hurting him too badly.

"Kenneth, I have something to confess." Hannah looked deep into his brown eyes and took a steadying breath. "You're a good man, and you deserve better. I'm afraid I can't offer anything more than friendship."

"Nonsense, I..."

"Please, let me finish. Several months ago, we made a date. Do you remember?" After he nodded, she continued. "But when you came by to pick me up, my mother told you I was sick?"

Kenneth nodded, looking confused. "Yes."

"I wasn't. I was out with another man. I had forgotten all about our date."

The expression of his face made him look like she had just run over his puppy. "Who?"

Hannah took a deep breath. "Mathew Stephens."

"Wait a minute..." He looked puzzled. "I know that name." A long moment of silence passed. "I remember," he blurted. "There are rumors going around that he is with the KKK." He stared at her, his eyes widening. "You like him? When did this happen?"

"I'm sorry," she said quietly, hurrying to add, "I met him one day by the lake on his property. At the time, I didn't know about the rumors."

Kenneth clenched his fists, anger written across his gentle features. "So you dissed me for some white man?"

Hannah shook her head, trying to calm his anger. "It wasn't like that."

"Then what is it like?" he exploded, moving away from her as if afraid she might give him some infectious disease. "I can't believe it. The whole time you were playing me for a fool."

"No, I wasn't," she argued, her cheeks heating with shame. "I had just met him, and before I knew what was happening, he had stolen my heart."

"If he is a member of the Klan, he hates our people. How could you possibly want anything to do with that racist, murdering pig? Surely you heard the same rumors I did." Kenneth's voice rose, echoing within the confines of the vehicle.

Hannah wanted to jump out of the car and run, but she owed it to Kenneth to stay.

He finally calmed down. "Do you love him?"

Her chest tightened with pain, and she blurted out, "I don't want to talk about him right now." Suddenly, she couldn't move, couldn't breathe, as if the world had constricted around her, holding her bound to this place and time.

He stared at her, his eyes glistening. "You know, when I returned home yesterday, I came back because I thought I had left something important behind in this little town."

"What's that?" She knew what he would say before his lips formed the words.

"You. I loved you, Hannah, even though we've never been together. I admired the person I thought you were – smart, funny, beautiful." His voice cracked, and he stopped, dragging in deep breaths like a marathon runner who had just completed a race.

Silence stretched between them, so taut that Hannah felt it would cut her if she spoke.

After a moment, he put his seatbelt on and started the car, anger and regret fighting for dominance on his dark face. He said nothing, and Hannah didn't know how to fix things between them. She had never realized that Kenneth had held such strong feelings for her. Truthfully, she had never wanted to know. And he had earned the right to hurt her back, but it didn't make her heart ache any less.

He drove her home, but did not get out of the car, or even turn his head when they pulled into the driveway. Without a word, she got out and shut the door. Almost before her hand left the handle, he backed out and drove away.

Her mother sat in the cozy living room, reading the latest Janet Evanovich novel and laughing at the latest crazy antics of Stephanie Plum, Lulu, and Grandma Mazur. Hannah dropped down next to her on the overstuffed couch, longing for her mother's warm comfort. Deborah Collins marked her place, laid the book aside, and opened her arms. With a cry, Hannah allowed herself to be pulled in her mother's embrace as the tears, she had been fighting all night, overwhelmed her.

Deborah let her cry, holding her and whispering words of comfort. When Hannah could speak without sobbing, she sat back, taking one of her mother's hands.

"I can't believe he hurt me, Ma."

Her mother's eyes flashed with concern. "Kenneth hurt you?"

"Not Kenneth," Hannah said, struggling to hold back fresh tears at the memory of Kenneth's face and the loss of his love. "Mathew."

"Are you still thinking about that rotten white man?" Her mother's frown scolded her.

"I can't believe he would try to kill Daddy, or anyone else," Hannah sniffed. "The man I love... the man I gave myself to... I've tried to stop loving him. I tried to turn that love to hate... but I can't, ma. I just can't."

Her mother reached out her free hand and smoothed her daughter's hair. "Hannah, baby, you gave yourself to him because you were lonely."

"It wasn't that. I don't fall in love easily," she said. "There was just something about Mathew."

Hannah's father walked in on their conversation, his face darkening at the mention of Mathew's name.

"You think you love that son-of-a-bitch?" he growled. "That man wanted to kill me. I don't want you to ever speak his name in front of your mother or me again. You hear me, girl?"

Without waiting for her answer, he turned and left the room. A few seconds later, a door slammed upstairs.

Mrs. Collins turned to her daughter. "It will be all right, baby."

Hannah buried herself in her mother's arms.

Chapter Twenty-One

Geoff stepped outside to retrieve the newspaper from his front porch and found an envelope tucked inside. He looked up and down the street and then back at the envelope. It did not have a stamp, and the mailman was nowhere in sight, so he took the paper and the envelope inside. His policeman's instincts kicked in. Carrying the items into his office, he laid them on his desk and grabbed a pair of disposable gloves from the right-hand desk drawer. Pulling them on, he slipped the envelope out from the newspaper and carefully slit it open with a letter opener, pulling out a single piece of paper that had words made from letters cut from magazines and newspapers. It read, "You are next."

Geoff had a pretty good idea what the ominous note meant. He took a plastic baggie from the kitchen and stuck the paper and envelope inside in case fingerprints had been left on the paper, but he doubted it. Someone knocked at his door. Opening it, he found an officer waiting on the porch.

"You're needed at the station, sir."

Unsettled by the seriousness of the officer's demeanor, Geoff hesitated. "Sure," he said, turning to grab his jacket. "What's up?"

"It's Chief Waldron, sir. He's been shot."

Geoff stuffed the bag with the note into his pocket and sprinted to the patrol car. "Skip the station. Take me to the scene. Now!"

The officer switched on his siren and sped toward the Chief's house.

Geoff yanked his cell phone out of his jacket pocket and called Rosie. She would wonder what had happened to him, and he did not want her to worry.

"Geoff, what's wrong?" she answered, alarm in her voice.

"Sorry, I had to run out without telling you, Rosie. The Chief has been shot."

"Oh, no," she cried. "Is he dead?"

"I don't know yet. This is too much – first Danny, and now the Chief. Honey, this is getting crazy."

"You be careful, Geoff," she said.

"I will, honey." He now knew for certain the meaning of the note and was thankful that Rosie hadn't found it first.

When Geoff arrived at the Chief's house, he flashed his badge at the tape barrier and hurried inside. Two street cops stood in the big living room, as a younger police officer Geoff didn't know leaned out an open window and threw up.

Officer Stone looked up as Geoff walked in, straightening as he recognized him. Geoff didn't take time for pleasantries.

"Where's the Chief?"

"He's in the bedroom over there." The officer pointed to an open doorway down a short carpeted hallway.

The Lieutenant's footsteps were heavy and silent on the beige rug as he forced himself to walk toward the room. He knew exactly what he would find even before he reached the bedroom.

"This can't be happening," he muttered, steeling himself to enter the open doorway. The telltale coppery stench of stale blood hit him as he neared the room.

The Chief, dressed in pajamas, his feet bare, lay across his bed with a bullet hole in his lower jaw. The pillows, bedside table, and nearby wall were splattered with congealing blood and brain matter that had sprayed in thick gouts as the projectile exited, taking the top of his head with it. From his vantage point, Geoff noticed the shotgun near the Chief's out-flung hand. He turned and walked out of the room, fighting to keep his breakfast down.

"What have you got?" he barked at the officer closest to him. The man's nametag read M. Graham.

"The crime scene unit is on their way," the man told him. "We didn't want to touch anything until they're finished, and the coroner removes the... body."

Geoff pulled out his handkerchief and wiped his sweaty face, breathing deeply. "Did you contact his daughter?" The Chief's wife had died from lung cancer five years ago.

"No, sir," Graham told him, using a Kleenex to wipe his own pale face. "I figured a ranking officer should notify her."

"You're correct. I'll head over to his daughter's house to break the news before the media arrives. In the meantime, let's get the crime scene guys going so we can get the Chief's body out of here."

Graham nodded, and hurried out the front door. Geoff followed him. He needed a breath of fresh air and desperately wished that Danny was alive.

Danny's partner, Jim Tyler, a short, slender man with wavy black hair and blue eyes, pulled up in an unmarked car, walked up, and placed a hand on Geoff's shoulder. "Will I do?" he asked softly, as if he knew what Geoff was thinking.

Geoff nodded.

Jim pulled on a pair of disposable gloves and walked into the bedroom without looking at the Chief's body. Instead, he went to the window, which had been opened just a crack. Geoff watched as he examined every detail of the frame and lock.

"The window's been tampered with," Jim said. Turning back to the room, he moved to the foot of the Chief's bed and examined the body and surrounding area. For several minutes, he said nothing, but Geoff saw his hands tighten into fists. "Who did this?"

The words were so soft, Geoff thought for a moment he had imagined them, until he saw the anger in Jim's eyes. He walked over and placed a hand on the other man's arm, gently drawing him away from the body on the bed. "We'll find them, Jim. We'll make them pay – for the Chief and for Danny."

Jim glanced at him, anger mixed with pain on his face. "There is a price to pay for everything, Geoff. Someone had to pay for letting people know who those bastards are. That's the price we pay for the love of our job, for the love of justice. You never get something for nothing."

Geoff stared at him. "You're not saying the Chief deserved this, are you?"

"No," Jim said. "I'm just saying there are consequences for everything we do, good or bad."

"Someone tried to make it look like a suicide," Geoff said.

"I noticed that, but there is no way the Chief would do that."

"I agree. Be sure and tell the coroner to send the Chief's blood to the lab. Someone either drugged him first or knocked him out. Otherwise they would never have been able to shoot him that way. The Chief always said he was a light sleeper, so I doubt they could have sneaked up on him and done it while he was asleep."

Geoff looked up as the forensics team hurried into the room, and motioned for Jim to follow him into the living room.

"Let's let forensics do their job. We have other matters to attend to."

George O'Connor, a middle-aged man with chiseled features, entered the house and was directed to the bedroom as they were leaving. As the local funeral home director, as well as coroner and forensics expert, he wore a black suit and silvery gray tie. He stopped them in the living room before heading to the bedroom.

"Morning Lieutenant... Detective." He nodded at them both and reached into his bag for a pair of latex gloves, before looking up, his grey eyes solemn.

"The Chief was a close friend. I'll take good care of him."Geoff nodded and left to deliver the devastating news to the Chief's daughter.

Chapter Twenty-Two

When Hannah arrived at her office early Monday morning, she picked up the mail and hurried to her desk, dropping the stack near her keyboard. It wasn't until an hour later, while taking a coffee break, that she noticed the top envelope. It was hand-addressed, and she thought it was Mathew's handwriting. She reached for it, and then hesitated. If it was from Mathew, could she bear to read it?

She left the envelope untouched and tried to get back to work, but the letter seemed to taunt her from its place on the desk, distracting her thoughts. Finally, with a sigh, she gave up and reached for it again, pulling a single sheet of paper from the envelope. It confirmed her fears. Mathew was still trying to reach her; even though she had made it perfectly clear by her silence that she wanted nothing more to do with him.

The letter read:

Dear Hannah,

I hope this finds you in good spirits. I never stop thinking of you. The Klansmen learned of our relationship, and I didn't deny it, couldn't deny the depth of my feelings for you. It's been pretty rough. My life has been threatened, and I suppose that is its own form of justice.

I am truly sorry for the lies I told you. Here is the truth. I was a proud Klansmen until I met you. The night you cooked that fish dinner for me, I fell in love with you, and I realized for the first time in my life how wrong I had been to think that your people were any different from mine. I admit. It was a shock, one I wrestled with for many days as I tried to reconcile my love for a woman of color against the hatred I had wrongfully harbored for Negros. It shook me up, Hannah, more than you will ever realize. And the wrongs I had committed stabbed me in the gut like a burning poker.

I was so wrong... so stupid, but falling in love with you, and meeting your wonderful parents showed me what a complete idiot I have been. I hope you can find it in your heart to forgive me and maybe... give me another chance. Think about our very first kiss and all its passion.

I am a changed man, Hannah. During my life, I have known physical fear, and now I have learned emotional fear. I'm afraid I have forever lost you, and that our love will never be allowed to grow and blossom into the gentle flower that sprouted that day by the lake. Please, give me another chance.

I love you.
Mathew Stephens

She crumpled the letter in her hand, wishing she could do the same with the love he had offered. Still, something stirred within her at the memory of their first kiss, the intense passion of their lovemaking, and the depth of her feelings for him. She had believed in him, wanted him more than any man she had ever known, until she discovered the truth. No matter what he said, her heart would never forgive him.

She looked down at the letter, smoothing it out on the desk blotter before refolding and returning it to the envelope. Somehow, she couldn't bring herself to destroy it, despite the emotions raging within her mind. Someday, she would find the courage to kill the last spark of love hiding deep within her soul.

At five-fifteen, after losing herself in work all day, Hannah realized it was time to head home. She quickly packed her briefcase and rushed out of the office.

As she headed for her car, a stranger bumped into her, knocking her hard against a parked Camry.

"Ow!"

Gray Love

She looked up. The man stood at least a head taller. He gave her a cold stare from icy blue eyes, as if the contact had been intentional. As he moved past, Hannah noticed that his hair was dishwater blond, and he wore glasses. She wouldn't soon forget him. Collecting herself, she tried to brush aside a growing fear that stabbed her heart as she hurried to her car, locking the doors as soon as she got inside. She had to get home.

Her mother stood at the stove, a colorful cotton apron tied neatly around her waist.

"Hey, Ma," Hannah said, kissing her on the cheek. "Something smells good. What are you cooking?"

"Meatloaf, dear," her mother replied with a smile. "Why don't you take a nice warm bath and change before we eat?"

Hannah climbed the stairs to her room and started running the water for her bath. As the tub filled with warm soapy water, she undressed. Fishing in her dresser for clean underwear, she came across a picture of Mathew standing on the deck of his boat, smiling at the camera, his hair ruffled by the wind. She had taken the picture months earlier. Hannah ran her index finger across the surface as if gently caressing his face, then tucked the picture back into the drawer and went into the bathroom. No matter how hard she tried, it seemed there would always be something to remind her of him.

Steam surrounded her, and she fought the sudden urge to vomit. After reaching across the tub to open the window and let in some fresh air, she perched on the edge of the bathtub and took several deep breaths of the cooler air, before sliding into the warm, sudsy water.

An hour later when Hannah came downstairs for dinner, she found that her mother had set the table and was placing a platter of meatloaf next to a bowl of steaming mashed potatoes, buttered carrots, and freshly baked rolls. Her father said grace, and while they ate, they talked about their day and things that still needed to be done. After they finished eating and put everything away, Hannah thought of her unfinished case studies, but she didn't feel like working and decided to spend the evening with her parents.

Her mother served warm apple pie with cinnamon ice cream on the side for dessert. As Hannah lifted the first forkful to her mouth, a car's headlights lit their driveway. Her parents both looked at her.

"Are you expecting someone tonight?" her mother asked.

"No, I'm not." Hannah's eyes widened with fear as she looked across the table at her father and lowered her fork.

"You two sit still," Mr. Collins said, turning off the kitchen light. He hurried into the living room and gently pushed aside the curtain an inch to peek out the front picture window. Hannah watched his hands clench. She joined him, looking over his shoulder. Two figures in ghostly robes stood in the driveway, facing the front door.

"Go upstairs," he commanded, turning to frown at her.

From doorway between the kitchen and living room, Hannah's mother asked, "Charlie, what's the matter?"

Her father glanced over his shoulder, his face tight with anger and fear. "I said get upstairs now."

Hannah grabbed her mother's arm and pulled her toward the steps.

"Call 911, hurry," she urged, pushing her mother upward. "I'll keep an eye on the back door."

Charlie went to the hall closet to get his rifle and loaded shells into it before boldly walking outside to confront the two intruders. Hannah could see and hear him clearly through the open door.

"Is there a problem?"

One man was a little over six feet tall and ruggedly built; the other was slightly overweight and his head came up to his partner's shoulders.

"Yeah, we have a problem with your daughter. We think your girl's been messing with things she shouldn't outta mess with."

"What my daughter does is none of your business," Charlie growled, hefting the rifle in both hands.

"She's been messing with a white boy, and that's unacceptable. Don't need no black trash pollutin' the bloodline."

Her father snorted. "Her relationships are none of your concern, so I think you had better get the hell away from here."

"What did you say, boy?" the taller man asked.

Mr. Collins raised his gun to aim it at them. "I won't give a warning shot like Taylor Henderson did. I'm aiming right at your maggot infested heart."

The shorter man stepped forward. "I think we need to teach this here boy a lesson. We ought to put him in his place."

Even from where she stood, Hannah heard the determination in her father's voice, and her heart swelled with pride and fear as she hurried into the living room.

"Get the hell off my property and leave my family alone."

The tallest man pulled a gun from behind his back and fired a shot that tore into the doorframe next to Charlie. Hannah's father jumped aside, dropping the rifle.

Hannah shoved open the screen door and stepped out on the front porch. She grabbed her father's weapon and aimed, placing her finger on the trigger with deadly intent and narrowing her eyes. The Klansmen must have realized she wouldn't hesitate to kill them. As she prepared to shoot, they quickly jumped into their car. The squealing of tires and smell of scorched rubber filled the air as they backed out and sped away. She fired anyway, knowing she couldn't hit them, but when the blast shattered the car's windshield, she felt better.

Grabbing her father's arm, she led him back inside just as Hannah's mother rushed down the stairs, phone in hand.

"The police are on their way."

"A lot of good that will do now," Charlie huffed. "Give me that phone."

He dialed the number of the police station and put it on speakerphone so he could reload his weapon while he talked. The operator asked who he needed to speak to, and he requested Chief Waldron.

Geoff answered the Chief's phone. "Lieutenant Tray."

"It's Charlie Collins," her father barked into the phone. "I need the Chief."

"Mr. Collins, what's wrong?" Even over the phone, Hannah could hear the concern in the Lieutenant's voice.

"Two Klansmen came to my house dressed in robes and talking trouble," Charlie said, sliding a bullet into the rifle's chamber. "They mouthed off about my daughter and threatened me until she put bullet through their windshield."

"Your daughter put a... Why were they after her?"

Charlie slid a glance at Hannah, and then turned away to answer. "They're upset because she dated that Mathew Stephens a while back."

"Mathew Stephens?"

Hannah felt warmth creeping over her skin.

"Yes, Mathew Stephens," Mr. Collins snapped. "I'm worried for my family's safety. I want to talk to the Chief."

A long moment of silence answered him, then Geoff said, "I'm sorry, Mr. Collins, but the Chief is dead. He died under suspicious circumstances last night. It's all over the news."

"Oh, my God," Mr. Collins said. He looked from his wife to Hannah, his face paling.

"I suggest you stay inside tonight. I'll send a patrol car over to keep an eye on your place while we try to figure out who's behind this," Geoff said. "What kind of car were they driving?"

"A beat-up minivan, but the license plate was smeared with mud, so I can't tell you what was on it."

"All right, Mr. Collins, keep me informed."

"I will," Charlie replied, his shoulders drooping.

Her father hung up, and laid his rifle on the table.

Deborah wrapped her arms around her husband. "Thank God you're okay. I don't know what I would do without you."

"Hannah, don't you ever do that again," Charlie said, turning to his daughter, his eyes issuing a warning as well as containing a respect she had never before seen.

"Okay, Daddy, but I wasn't going to let them take another shot at you." Her lips trembled, and she realized how close she had come to losing him because of Mathew. Hannah smiled bravely at her father, blinking back the moisture in her eyes. Her parents needed some time alone, and so did she. "I think I'll go to my room and call it a night."

Her parents kissed her goodnight and reminded her to lock the bedroom door, just in case. Charlie checked the doors and windows to make sure they were locked as she climbed the steps to her room.

Later, wearing a fresh nightgown, Hannah got down on her knees next to her bed and prayed. "Dear Lord, please protect my family and all those I hold dear in my heart. I ask this in the name of Jesus Christ our Lord. Amen."

She climbed into bed and turned over, trying not to think about the events of the evening, but images of the wonderful days she had spent with Mathew kept running through her head like an old movie, keeping sleep at bay.

She rolled around restlessly for almost an hour before finally falling asleep. Her dreams filled with visions of Mathew pleading for mercy at the hands of his former friends, and begging her to help him.

Chapter Twenty-Three

Geoff received an early morning call from the coroner, after which he phoned Jim to tell him that the autopsy results were ready. They agreed to meet at the coroner's office. When Geoff arrived, he found Jim waiting for him, and together they walked into Dr. O'Connor's office.

Dispensing with pleasantries, Geoff asked, "What's the verdict, Dr. O'Connor?"

The coroner opened the file cabinet next to his desk and pulled out a slim folder. Taking a pair of wire-rimmed reading glasses from the pocket of his white lab coat, the doctor perched on the corner of his battered desk and pointed to the chairs in front of him.

"Would you gentleman care to have a seat?"

Geoff and Jim hesitated at first, but then sat down together. "Thanks," Geoff said politely.

Without further comment, the coroner opened the file and glanced at the contents. "The way the Chief was shot makes this look like a suicide."

Geoff gripped the arms of his chair, wanting to jump up and shout at the man that Waldron would never have done something like that, especially with the KKK situation hanging over his head.

The coroner peered over the top of his glasses for a moment, as if waiting for his words to sink in, and went on.

"Fortunately... the shotgun left on the bed is too long for the Chief to have pulled the trigger himself."

Geoff nodded. He hadn't really needed the coroner to confirm his suspicions. Ron Waldron had a daughter and grandchildren to live for. He had wanted to make his community a safer place and would have gone down fighting.

"So I'm ruling his death a homicide," the coroner said grimly.

"How did the perp subdue him?" Geoff asked.

"The killer must have sneaked in on Waldron while he was asleep."

"I don't get it. The Chief told me once that he was a light sleeper." Geoff had a puzzled look on his face.

"Maybe so, but he's been having a problem with insomnia this past month and was taking Lunesta. The crime scene techs found a prescription bottle in his medicine cabinet. He probably never knew what hit him."

"Makes sense," Jim said.

"You boys have your work cut out for you."

Geoff stood up and shook the coroner's hand, thanking him for his time. As they left the building, he and Jim walked to the car in silence. As they headed back to the precinct, Jim sighed.

"The Chief was a good man. It's going to be hard to replace him."

"Yes, he was the best." Geoff took a deep breath. "And I'm going to make sure whoever did this doesn't get away with it, if it's the last thing I do."

"Have forensics finished their report yet?" Jim asked.

"Not yet, however, they did say that the only gunshot residue was on the Chief's face and pajamas, but none on his hands," Geoff confirmed. "Whoever tried to make it look like a suicide was either stupid or very sloppy."

After leaving the coroner's office, the two officers headed for the Chief's neighborhood. They would interview the neighbors in hopes of finding someone who might have seen something the night of the murder. They tried the house on the right and the one across the street, but no one was home. So

Gray Love

they headed for the building on the left-hand side. The two detectives walked up the steps and onto the porch. The invigorating aroma of brewing coffee greeted them, and Jim nodded hopefully at the Lieutenant as he knocked on the door. They heard footsteps moving toward the door, and a short pause before the portal opened to reveal an elderly woman with short, curly white hair and lively brown eyes, wearing a red and white flowered housedress.

"Yes?"

"Good morning, ma'am," Jim greeted her. "I'm Detective Jim Tyler, and this is Lieutenant Geoff Tray of the Crystal Springs Police Department."

"Good morning, officers. What can I do for you?" she asked, a smile brightening her wrinkled face.

"We would like to ask you a few questions about the other night," Jim said.

"I'm Lucy Ketchins." She opened her door a bit wider, her expression troubled. "What kind of questions?"

"We're just checking around the neighborhood to see if anyone heard or saw anything the night Chief Waldron died, anything that might have seemed strange or unusual," Geoff said.

"It was a horrible incident," she exclaimed. "We all loved him. I can't believe he's dead. Poor man, he's been awfully lonely since Emma passed. His wife was always so nice and helpful. Whenever she went to the store, she always stopped by and asked if I needed anything. Most people these days don't bother with their neighbors, especially the elderly ones."

Geoff nodded. "No ma'am, they don't. Did you notice anything different that night, any unusual noises or strangers in the neighborhood?"

"Why don't you fine gentlemen come in for some coffee. I just brewed a fresh pot."

She unlocked the screen door and opened it wide, leading the officers into a small living room filled with an overstuffed sofa and matching chairs and maple end tables holding ginger jar lamps and inexpensive knickknacks of cats and dogs. A fat, long-haired tiger cat was curled up in one of the chairs. It opened its large yellow eyes to give them the once over, and finding nothing of interest, laid its head on its front paws and went back to sleep.

"Have a seat while I fetch the coffee," she said, motioning them to the navy blue couch. "Cream? Sugar?"

"Black is fine, ma'am," Geoff replied.

"Cream in mine, thanks," Jeff added.

Geoff looked around the room. The faded furniture and old-fashioned lamps complemented dark burgundy wallpaper decorated with huge cabbage roses. On one wall, neat rows of pictures hung, showing family groupings and several pictures of the woman who had answered the door at various stages of her life, usually accompanied by a stern-looking man.

The woman came back with a tray holding three cups of coffee, sugar, creamer napkins, spoons, and a coffee cake neatly sliced into precise little pieces. Geoff hurried to take the tray from her frail hands and placed it carefully on the coffee table.

"Thank you," she said, smiling. "Have a piece of that coffee cake. I just baked it this morning and it's still warm."

Jeff handed a cup of black coffee to the Lieutenant, and then picked up his own cup as both men politely refused the cake. Mrs. Ketchins added cream and sugar to hers.

"I like the pictures," Jeff said, sitting down and stirring cream into his coffee.

"Thank you," she replied, seating herself primly on a chair opposite the sofa. She took a sip of coffee before setting the cup and saucer on the end table next to her and folding her blue veined hands in her lap.

Gray Love

"The gentleman I'm hugging in those pictures is my husband." she lowered her voice. "I'm afraid he is quite ill now, so he's sleeping."

"I'm sorry to hear that." Geoff said, wondering how long the two had been married. He couldn't imagine what it would be like to watch someone you had been married to for so long, fade away.

"Don't feel bad," she said with a chuckle. "I'm just happy to keep him with me for as long as the Good Lord allows."

For a moment, both men sipped their coffee, and the room grew quiet except for the loud ticking of a grandfather clock that sat in the corner of the room. Finally, Jim set his cup and saucer on the coffee table.

"Did you see or hear anything out of the ordinary that night?" Not wanting to waste too much time with so many neighbors yet to interview, Jim jumped straight to the reason for their visit.

She closed her eyes, as she searched her mind. "No, not that I can remember."

He kept going. "No strange noises? Nothing peculiar?"

She shook her head, looking back at them with concern etched in her features. "No, I crawled into bed with my husband around nine-thirty and fell asleep. I'm a heavy sleeper, so I don't recall anything. To be perfectly honest, they could have been having a wild party next door, and I wouldn't have heard a thing."

Jim sat back on the couch, a disappointed expression on his face, as Geoff took up the questioning. "Is there any chance your husband might have noticed something?"

"I don't think so," she answered, reaching forward to put the lid back on the sugar bowl. "I'm certain he would have mentioned it if he had."

Geoff's heart sank. This would probably be the sum of their day, no one seeing or hearing anything the night the Chief was murdered. Still, he couldn't give up. "Did you wake up at any time during the night?"

Her face brightened for a moment. "Yes, come to think of it. I woke up around two in the morning. My husband was sleeping, but I knew he had been up earlier."

"And how did you know that, ma'am?" Geoff asked, leaning forward.

Her wrinkled cheeks flushed with rosy color, as if she wasn't used to discussing such matters with strangers. "When I went to the bathroom, the toilet seat was up. I always put it down before I retire. Don't want to accidently fall in now do I?"

"No ma'am. So sometime between nine-thirty and two a.m., your husband got up?" Jim asked excitedly.

She nodded again. "Yes. Are you sure you don't want to try a piece of my cake? It's very good."

"Thanks you, Mrs. Ketchins, I'm sure it is, but no. We just had breakfast. Would you mind if we looked around your home?"

"Not at all." She got up and reached for the coffee tray. "I'll just put these things away."

As she headed for the kitchen, she pointed down the hallway toward the bathroom in question. The officers hurried to the small bath painted white with green tiles on the walls and floor and looked out of the window. The Chief's bedroom window was directly across the way about ten feet.

"Perfect," Jim exclaimed. "Hey, Geoff, look at this. If Mr. Ketchins was up at the right time, he would have seen everything."

Geoff followed the Detective's gaze, noting the position of the window. They were close enough to see the fingerprint dust

Gray Love

on the Chief's windowsill. A moment later, the Lieutenant followed Jim out of the bathroom.

To the right of the bathroom, an open doorway led to the master bedroom. They saw Mr. Ketchins lying in the large four-poster bed, pale and gaunt against lavender-colored sheets. His wiry gray hair and wrinkled skin made him look at least eighty.

As soon as he saw them, the old man yelled for his wife. "Lucy!"

Mrs. Ketchins pushed past them and hurried into the room, wiping her hands on a dish towel. "What is it, dear?"

Mr. Ketchins pointed to Jim and Geoff standing outside his door.

She looked over at them with a smile, then turned back to place a reassuring hand on the old man's pajama sleeve. "These nice gentlemen are from the police. They're investigating the Chief's death."

"What do they want here?" His voice came out as a quiet croak, as if he hadn't spoken in a long time.

"They just wanted to know if we saw anything that night," she said, leaning down to brush the hair away from his left temple. He moved restlessly in the bed, his thin body barely disturbing the covers.

"My apologies, sir," Geoff said, stepping into the room. "We didn't mean to upset you. Your wife told us you might have gotten up sometime during the night the Chief was murdered. Is that true?"

"Murdered?" Mrs. Ketchins was shocked as she turned her head to look at Geoff. "The news said they weren't sure how he died."

Mr. Ketchins opened his mouth, but they could barely hear his words. Both officers moved closer to the bed.

The old man tried again. "Yes, I went to the bathroom that night."

"Do you know what time it was?" Jim asked, pulling a notebook from his breast pocket.

"It was around twelve-thirty. I heard a commotion going on outside the window," Mr. Ketchins murmured. "I don't like to turn on the light when I use the bathroom at night, so I didn't worry about them seeing me. They looked like they might be trying to break in."

Geoff glanced over at Jim and asked, "What did you do?"

"I went back to bed," Mr. Ketchins said, his pale cheeks warming with a flush. "We don't poke our noses in anybody's business but our own. We stay out of trouble that way." His last words came out with a hint of defiance, and he glared up at them with watery blue eyes.

"You didn't think you should call the police?" Geoff tried to keep his voice calm, but inside he seethed, and he knew he would have to leave soon, or he would lose his temper. The Chief's death might have been avoided if this man had only bothered to make a simple phone call.

"I told you," Mr. Ketchins muttered, his thin hands clutching the blankets covering him, "we stay to ourselves, and we stay safe. I'm too old to have to deal with a bunch of hooligans."

Jim touched Geoff's arm, urging him back toward the door. Geoff moved reluctantly, stopping for one last question.

"Can you describe the men you saw?"

"Nope. It was too dark to make out any details. The Chief's got plenty of guns in that house. I figured he could take care of himself."

"Well, if you remember anything else, please give us a call." Geoff reached into his pocket, retrieved a business card, and laid it on the dresser by the door.

Mr. Ketchins cleared his throat. "I will," he said.

At the door of the room, Jim turned back and asked, "Did you see a car or anything?"

The man nodded again. "I did, but like I said, it was too dark. Couldn't make out what type or color it was."

Mrs. Ketchins escorted them to the front door.

They thanked her and headed back to their car. Geoff slammed his door with unnecessary force as Jim settled into the passenger seat, saying nothing as he waited for the Lieutenant to blow off steam and get it off his chest.

"Dammit! A lousy phone call!" Geoff growled, punching the padded dash. "One fucking phone call and the Chief might still be alive. What is it with people like that?"

"Think about it, Geoff," Jim said quietly. "They're old and probably feel pretty vulnerable. You saw the man. He's in no shape to protect himself or anyone else. You can't blame them for not wanting to get involved. And now that I think about it, it's probably best they didn't. The way this case is going, I could just see the killers coming back and taking out the witnesses."

Geoff pounded the dash once more, his frustration struggling for release. "Hell, I know that, but they could have called it in anomalously. It might have saved the Chief's life."

Jim drew in a deep breath. "I know, but there's nothing we can do about that now. We'll just have to work with what we have."

"You bet I'll work with it," Geoff barked. Turning the key in the ignition, he quickly pulled away from the curb. "I want you to make a few calls and set up a press conference. It's time to get this community off their asses."

Chapter Twenty-Four

A couple of days later, Jim and Geoff got together to discuss how the case was progressing.

"We've got a lead," Jim said.

"Really?" Geoff asked, his hopes rising. "What kind of lead?"

"The appeal to the community brought in hundreds of phone calls and letters," Jim said. "I've waded through a ton of the stuff, and I believe I have found a solid lead. Walters is running it down as we speak."

"Don't keep me in suspense," Geoff said, settling on a corner of his desk.

"Remember Chris Thibodaux?" Jim watched for Geoff's reaction, and he wasn't disappointed as the other man scowled.

"The guy practically threw us off his property the other day and threatened to sue the department!" Geoff wrinkled his nose. "What an ass. If I had my way, I would have hauled him back to jail."

Jim smiled, enjoying the moment. They deserved it after all the heartache and anger over the Chief's death. It was about time they finally got a break.

"Right," he said. "We got a tip from a woman who said that Thibodaux purchased a shotgun and ammo just before the murder. I checked with the salesman that sold him the gun, and it's exactly like the one that killed the Chief."

Geoff abruptly stood up. "Why are we sitting around? Let's pick him up."

"Calm down, Lieutenant." Jim sighed. "We don't want to go off half-cocked and arrest him based solely on that fact.

Remember what happened the last time we locked up the Klan? I've asked the judge for a search warrant."

"Based on what? The judge is going to want more than a gun purchase before he agrees to a warrant. Beside, you don't think he still has it, do you?" Geoff dropped into his chair, but his expression remained angry and eager. "That would be pretty stupid."

Jim shrugged. "So how many smart criminals do you know? Why would he get rid of it? He has no idea we're on to him. Our vague statement to the press leaves Waldron's death open as to whether or not we believe it was a suicide. As far as he's concerned, no one saw what happened. Hell, we would still be in the dark if someone hadn't turned him in."

"Who phoned it in?" Geoff asked. "Do we know?"

Jim drew in a deep breath and shook his head. "It was an anonymous woman, who refused to leave her name. When we traced the number back, we discovered that she had called from a phone booth."

"Tomorrow after the funeral, I want to talk to Thibodeaux," Geoff muttered.

"I knew you would say that." Jim said. "Maybe we can even get him to invite us inside. Want some company?"

* * *

The morning of the funeral, more than half the town was packed inside the Roses Funeral Home to mourn the Chief. His daughter, dressed in a black two-piece suit with a diamond cross resting against her bosom, sobbed openly in her husband's arms from the first row, unable to look at the coffin in the front of the room. Her children clung to their grandparents, crying and uncertain what was happening. They did not understand why their other grandfather didn't wake up and play with them.

Hannah was there with her family, and recognized many of the people. Geoff Tray and his wife, and most of the police force, including several deputies from the Sheriff's Department who were friends of the Chief's, were present, making two unbroken rows of uniforms and gleaming silver badges. Beautiful arrangements of lilies, roses and baby's breath decorated the top of the casket next to a picture of the Chief, his broad face smiling.

Samuel Hugh Johnson led the service, a brown, heavyset man who had known the Chief and his family for many years. Two associate ministers joined Reverend Johnson at the tiny pulpit provided by the funeral home. The minister began the service by singing a brief hymn he had written as a tribute to the Chief.

"Walk to Jesus, my sweet Jesus, as you travel on your way. We pray you make it back to Heaven from where you came."

His deep voice resonated through the crowd, evoking tears and sobs from those attending.

After the song, he read short verses from the Bible, regarding the soul's passage to Heaven. He preached about how death is really a rebirth, and that he hoped it would be somewhat of a consolation to Elizabeth Perkins, the Chief's grieving daughter and her family. When he finished, he called upon Elizabeth to say a few words about her father.

Elizabeth slowly walked toward the pulpit, briefly stopping to lay a hand on the casket as she passed. For several seconds, she seemed to struggle with her grief, but after taking a deep, shuddering breath, she lifted her chin and faced the crowd.

"My father was a good man who helped anyone who came to him. He never judged or turned anyone away."

People in the crowd nodded.

"Most of all, he was a good father and grandfather," she continued. "When I was a little girl, I had a fish named Spike."

She smiled, her eyes distant. "Spike was a white fish with a weird-looking green line that ran the length of his body. One day, I came home from school and found him floating at the top of his little tank. I was devastated. Daddy knew how I felt about Spike. So that day, he had visited every shop in the community that sold fish, trying to find one that looked exactly like Spike. But he couldn't find one with the same green line. Later that week, I came home from school and caught him trying to draw a green line on this poor little white fish with a permanent marker."

The crowd murmured, and several laughed aloud.

"I loved him so much. He always tried his best to make me happy."

She spoke proudly of her father's accomplishments as a police officer, and his journey in the office from a green rookie to his final rank as Chief. When she finished, she walked back to her father's coffin and rested her right hand on it.

"I will never forget you, Daddy. At least you and Mom are together at last."

She stood there for several moments, her shoulders shaking, until her husband gently escorted her back to her seat. Elizabeth resisted at first, but then collapsed against him and allowed him to lead her away.

Reverend Johnson said a final prayer, and quiet sobs filled the funeral home. After the prayer, the preacher stepped over to the coffin, opened his arms wide, and faced the crowd. "Let us prepare for burial."

Elizabeth rose from her seat as the casket passed, falling into step behind it, still supported by her husband in his dark gray suit. Six high-ranking officers from the Sheriff's Department, dressed in full dress uniform, carried the casket outside to the waiting hearse.

The preacher led the line, singing. "Walk with Jesus, my sweet Jesus, as I lay my burden down. Fly to Jesus, oh, sweet Jesus until you're home."

Elizabeth and her family climbed into the black limousine, parked behind the hearse. A long trail of cars had already lined up to follow. At the cemetery, Elizabeth looked around, her dark eyes red-rimmed from crying. Hannah's heart went out to her, and she wanted to hug the other woman and promise her anything to make her feel better. But she moved to the side, with her family. Hugs and words of sympathy could wait until the graveside prayers had been concluded.

The preacher blessed the Chief one more time before they lowered his coffin into the ground. Elizabeth kissed a long-stemmed red rose, laying it gently across the casket.

"I love you, Daddy," she whispered as Hannah came up behind her.

When Hannah and her parents returned home from the funeral, she went upstairs and sat on her bed. How could anyone do such a thing to the Chief and his family?

Her mother came into her room and kissed the top of Hannah's head.

"Everything will be all right." She paused. "I can sense how sad you are, and I don't think it's just because of the Chief. I remember how happy you were every time you saw Mathew, and I think you miss him a lot."

Hannah shot her mother a surprised look.

"Don't look at me like that, girl." Her mother smiled. "I'm not blind."

Hannah stood and gave her mother a hug. "Thanks, Ma," she said, trying to look a bit happier.

"You're welcome, dear," Mrs. Collins said. "I'm going downstairs to talk to your father. Why don't you try to rest a bit?"

"I will," Hannah promised. She watched as her mother walked out of the room before lying back on the bed. She had been feeling sick all day, nauseous and sweaty, and that morning before the funeral, she had made a doctor's appointment for the next day. She already knew she was pregnant, but wanted the doctor to confirm it. And then, she would have to tell her parents.

* * *

Early Saturday morning, Geoff and Jim drove to Chris Thibodaux's home. A beat-up minivan was parked next to his small, frame house in a driveway that ran around the back of the building. The license plate was still covered with mud.

Geoff looked around, assessing the situation. "You go around back, and I'll take the front."

Jim nodded, removing his weapon from its holster. "You got it," he said. "I'll see you on the other side." He got out of the car.

Geoff watched Jim move stealthily past the minivan and disappear into the dawn shadows. Jeff slipped noiselessly from the car, softly closing the door behind him, before carefully climbing the front porch steps and knocking on the door.

After several minutes, a woman opened the door a crack, one hand holding the door, and the other clutching a red flannel robe tight against her bosom.

"What do you want?"

Geoff flashed his badge. "I'm Lieutenant Geoffrey Tray of the Crystal Springs Police Department. I need to speak with Chris Thibodaux," he said with his best professional smile.

"He's not here." The woman glanced to the side and then back at Geoff.

The move raised the hair on the back of his neck. "Ma'am, I need to come inside," he said firmly. He moved forward, but she blocked his path.

"You can't," she insisted, her fingers whitening as she clutched the edge of the door.

Geoff reached for the door. "Please step aside, ma'am." His other hand slid down to his weapon, slipping off the holster guard.

A commotion at the back of the house brought his head around, but not before he saw the panic on the woman's face.

Geoff heard Jim yell. "Get down on the ground."

Two shots blasted the early morning silence. Geoff jumped off the porch and ran toward the back of the house, pulling his weapon in one smooth movement. The woman hurried after him.

A man lay writhing on the ground as Jim stood over him, weapon ready.

"What happened?"

"He took a shot at me," Jim calmly replied. "I told him to drop it and get down, but he kept running, so I shot him in the foot. Don't worry; the bastard will live."

"Have you read him his rights?" Geoff asked.

"Yup, while I was cuffing him," Jim replied.

Geoff looked down at the wounded man. "Are you Chris Thibodeaux?" His voice was soft with no hint of threat.

"He shot me!" the prisoner moaned, as he rocked back and forth on the ground.

"Answer the man's question," Jim barked.

"So what if I am?"

"I'm going to ask one more time, sir. Are you Chris Thibodeaux?"

"Yeah, that's me," Thibodaux said, his voice sullen.

Gray Love

They pulled him to his feet and helped him limp around to the front of the house to the unmarked police car, where they placed him in the back seat.

Jim used his cell phone to call for an ambulance as the woman hurried toward the car, but Geoff put up a hand to stop her.

"Ma'am, please don't come any closer," he warned.

"I just want to make sure he's okay," she whined, trying to move around him.

Geoff stepped between her and the car again. "Ma'am, Mr. Thibodeaux is under arrest for the murder of Chief Waldron. Please go back inside."

A shocked look crossed her face, but she didn't waste another moment. "I'm calling a lawyer." She hurried away, her back straight and rigid. She slammed the front door as soon as she stepped inside.

Jim rolled his eyes. When the ambulance arrived, they cuffed Thibodaux to the gurney for the ride to the hospital. Geoff called for an officer to meet the ambulance there, and they drove back to the station.

As he walked to his desk, the phone rang. The woman on the line sounded as if she were whispering.

"Hello, is this Lieutenant Geoffrey Tray?" She sounded anxious.

"Yes, this is Lieutenant Tray," he replied, moving around the desk to drop into his chair. "How can I help you?"

"I'm calling about the murder."

Geoff sat forward with a thump and reached for a notepad and pen. "Chief Waldron's murder?"

The lady continued in a soft voice. "Yes. I'm at work, and I don't want anyone to hear me. I think my husband is involved."

"What makes you think that?"

"The night Chief Waldron was murdered, my husband was out, and when he came home, he burned his clothes."

Geoff sucked in a breath. "Ma'am, what is your husband's name?"

The pause at the other end of the line was so long, Geoff thought she had hung up, but finally she said, "His name is Sky Frances."

He wrote the name on the pad and signaled to a nearby officer. "I need you to tell me what happened that night, whatever you know." He covered the receiver with his hand long enough to tell the officer, "Get Jim Tyler in here."

The woman started talking, the words gushing out as though she had bottled them up, waiting for someone to ask the right question. "He came home early in the morning that day. Chris Thibodeaux was with him. I'm used to him coming in drunk, but he took a shower, and he's never done that before."

"Go on." Geoff looked up, his heart beating hard. Finally, they would learn the truth.

"I know a shower's not strange," she went on, "but a few minutes after he turned off the water, I smelled smoke." She paused again. "I looked out the window, and my husband and Chris were in the back yard, both in their underwear, burning what looked like the clothes they'd had on earlier." Her voice rose a bit with what sounded like displeasure. "That Chris Thibodaux is a bad influence. I just knew they had been up to no good."

Geoff's hand flew across the page, making notes as fast as he could.

"If you want proof, check the fire barrel in my back yard," she added. "Sky's out of town today, so no one will bother you."

"Thank you, Mrs. Frances," Geoff said. "We'll be in touch."

As he hung up the phone, Jim walked in.

"What's up?" he asked.

"A woman claiming to be the wife of Sky Frances just called to say that she believes her husband and Chris Thibodaux murdered the Chief. She suggested we check the trash barrel behind their house where her husband and Thibodaux burned the clothes they were wearing the night the Chief was killed."

Jim frowned. "If they're burned, how will that help us?"

"There might be something left to help us pin the murder on them," Geoff said. He got up from his desk. "I'm heading over there."

"Let's let forensics handle that while we talk to Thibodaux." Jim hurried out of the office, Geoff close behind. They notified forensics to check out the back yard of the Frances' home, and left for the hospital.

Thibodeaux was in the emergency room, getting his foot bandaged as the bullet had only nicked him. A uniformed officer stood near the door. The nurse looked up questioningly as they pushed past the curtain, but moved aside when they flashed their badges.

Geoff stood next to the bed, watching Thibodeaux pull against the handcuffs holding him to the bed rail. "Okay, Chris, why did you do it?"

Thibodaux looked up at him, then over to Jim, as if he was too good to talk to Geoff. "I don't know what you're talking about. I was home that night."

Jim stared right back at him. "That night? What night are you referring to, Chris?"

Thibodeaux blanched as he stammered his reply. "You know… the night you… you asked about."

"I never mentioned a specific night, so it must be your guilty conscience speaking. I'm talking about the night Chief Waldron was murdered. You're in trouble, Chris, and now we know you had help."

Something flickered in the man's eyes, making Geoff smile. Thibodaux took a deep breath, and his sneer was back in place. "Still don't know what you're talking about."

Geoff leaned down, getting right in the man's face. "Listen, you little bastard. Don't mess with me. I'll have your ass rotting in the state penitentiary for the rest of your life."

Thibodaux glared at him. "Since when does a colored man get to be a lieutenant?"

"Since the rest of the world left the dark ages behind," Geoff grinned, stepping back. He knew he had gotten a rise the minute the racial slur surfaced. "Got a problem with that?"

"I ain't got no problems." Thibodaux fidgeted on the gurney. "And I ain't got nothing to say to either one of you. I don't know what the hell you're talking about."

Jim came up on the other side of the bed. "You know, since you're going down anyway, you might as well take your friend with you."

"I don't rat on friends," Thibodaux snapped. "We played cards and drank all night."

"I thought you said you were home all night." Jim looked across at Geoff. "So do you have an alibi?"

Chris hesitated for a second, before saying, "I was with Sky Frances. We were at his house the night the Chief died, playing cards and drinking. Just ask his wife."

"All night?"

"Yeah, all night."

"You seem to remember that night pretty well for someone who had spent the night drinking." Geoff smiled. "You couldn't have been too drunk."

"Sober enough to know I didn't do nothing wrong." Thibodaux kept his gaze on Jim, as if he could make Geoff disappear by not acknowledging at him. "And you didn't have to shoot me. I'm gonna sue both of you and the whole department."

Jim sighed. "Do whatever you gotta do. We're going to bring in Frances and see what he has to say. The first one to make a deal usually wins, you know."

Thibodaux rattled the handcuffs against the metal rail of the gurney. "Dammit, you leave us alone. We're good Americans, and don't deserve this kind of shit."

Geoff walked over to Jim so the other man would have to look at him. "Sure, sure, we've heard it all before. Anything else you want to say, save it for the judge."

"I want a lawyer!" Thibodeaux yelled after them.

"Yes, sir, Mr. Thibodeaux, I believe your wife said she was calling an attorney as soon as she went back inside the house. I'm sure he'll be waiting at the station for us."

As soon as the doctor was finished, the two officers left the emergency room with Thibodeaux in custody. Now, all they had to do was to wait for the crime scene unit to tell them what they had found at the Frances' home.

Chapter Twenty-Five

On Friday morning, Hannah was awakened from a deep sleep by the ringing of the telephone. She glanced at the clock and saw it was 6:30. "Damn, who's calling this early?"

"Hannah, it's for you," her mother called from the master bedroom. "I can't make out who it is."

Hannah picked up her phone. "Hello?"

"Hannah, please don't hang up."

Hannah struggled to sit up in bed, her stomach tightening. "Mathew?"

"How are you doing?"

She leaned back against her headboard and drew the sheets up around her. "What do you want, Mathew?"

A short silence, then, "I would really like to see you." Mathew's low voice held hope and fear.

She pressed a hand against her stomach, wishing she could trust him... tell him her secrets. "I can't forgive you, Mathew. I'm sorry. I don't ever want to see or hear from you again."

She dropped the receiver into the cradle, tears welling in her eyes. How dare he call her and stir up old feelings, just when she thought she was getting her life back on track? And why couldn't she let go of the anger and the love warring within her heart? The small hope his voice had given her, when she first answered the phone, struggled against the tide of anger and died a quick, painful death. For a long time now, she had known her life would never be the same.

"Are you all right?" Her mother's soft voice came from the doorway.

Hannah looked up, and the tears she had been holding back streamed down her cheeks. With a soft cry, her mother hurried to the bed and gathered Hannah into her arms.

"Cry, baby, cry all you want. Just let it all out."

For long moments, Hannah did just that. She cried as her heart broke, soothed by her mother's hand stroking her hair. She cried for everything she had lost, the love of a man she had thought was her soul mate, and the innocence of that love. She cried, because no matter how terrible Mathew had been, she still loved him. Hannah didn't know if she could ever rid herself of the feelings she had for the man who had planned to murder her father, especially since she was carrying his child. And now what would she do? She was pregnant, but she could never tell him, could never share the beauty of that reality.

"Ma?" she asked, her face still buried in her mother's arms.

"Yes, dear heart, what is it?"

"I don't know how to say this..." Hannah started.

"You still love him, don't you, Hannah?" her mother whispered against the top of her head.

Hannah nodded, but couldn't bring herself to say the words.

"Your Daddy and I want you to be happy, girl." Her mother's voice held compassion, and sadness. "And if you think your happiness lies with that white man, you have to make sure."

"What are you saying?" Hannah twisted upward to see her mother's face. The look there made her want to cry all over again.

"I'm saying that if you love someone, you have to give them a second chance."

Hannah started to speak, but her mother stopped her with a raised hand. "I know what he planned, and I know your father still carries hatred in his heart for him, but I also know he will forgive you and that man, if you are truly meant to be together. You just have to give him a little time."

"There's something I have to tell you, Ma," Hannah said, her voice calmer now that she had made a decision. "I'm carrying Mathew's child."

"I know, baby, I know." Her mother tightened her embrace.

"You know?" Hannah gasped. "How?"

"Mothers just know these things, dear. God gave us that sense."

"You think I should see him?" Hannah whispered, taking her mother's hand.

Deborah gave her daughter's hand a gentle squeeze. "I think he should know about the baby. You owe him that. And you owe yourself the chance to be happy, or to be rid of him once and for all. You can't do that if you won't face him. Unless you settle this once and for all, it'll hang around your heart like an anchor, forever pulling you down."

Hannah knew her mother was right. She would go to Mathew, talk to him, and find out if there was anything between them that could be salvaged. She hugged her mother. "I may never have told you this before, but you are a very wise woman."

Her mother smiled. "It's a shame I have to get this old to hear my child say that, isn't it?"

Chapter Twenty-Six

The forensic team found pieces of partially burned clothing containing blood spatter, and belonging to both Sky Frances and Chris Thibodaux. The blood's DNA was tested, and it matched the Chief's perfectly. The evidence was enough for a judge to grant them a search warrant for both homes, and after a thorough search, they found the shotgun used in the murder with Thibodaux's fingerprints all over it. Sky Frances was arrested as soon as he returned home from his trip. A month later, he and Chris Thibodaux stood trial for the murder of Chief Waldron. The trial lasted two days, with the defendants using the same attorney that had represented the KKK members in the earlier proceedings. The jury was out for three hours before returning a guilty verdict.

Geoff sat behind the prosecutor's table, a shiny new badge on his uniform jacket. He had been appointed Chief of Police and conscious of his new stature, he would see this trial finished for the man he had admired so much. As he waited for the sentencing to be pronounced, he silently prayed for those they had lost to racial violence like Chief Waldron, Danny Pummel, and Taylor Henderson. Ken Louis had been found guilty of murdering Taylor Henderson and was currently serving a life sentence in the same prison that would soon welcome Thibodaux and Frances.

This morning, the two defendants awaited sentencing from Judge Stone. They were brought into the courtroom, dressed in street clothes, wearing shackles on their wrists and ankles. Silence held the room in its grip as they made their way to the wooden table where their attorney waited. After they were seated, the bailiff called out, "All rise."

Judge Stone swept into the room, his black robe swirling around him. He did not look around until he was seated with a manila folder open on the bench in front of him. Frowning, he gazed across at the defense table as everyone returned to their seats.

"Sky Frances, please rise."

Frances rose from his seat, his bravado of the past few weeks completely gone. He wore an ill-fitting sports jacket over khaki pants, and his sparse gray hair lay dull and flat on his head. His wife Roberta sat behind him, but kept her head down, a look of relief on her face that this would soon be over. She had an appointment this afternoon with a highly recommended divorce lawyer and was relieved that she would never again have to put up with her husband's abuse.

The judge glanced at the papers before fixing his gaze on the man standing before him.

"Sky Frances, I hereby sentence you to life in a federal prison, with no possibility of parole, for the murder of Police Chief Ronald Waldron."

Geoff looked around the room, pleased with the sentence. A murmur raced through the crowd as the judge's gavel rapped the wooden disk on his desk.

Then the judge looked at Thibodaux. "Chris Thibodaux, please rise."

Thibodaux rose from his chair, standing awkwardly in a cheap black suit, his hair slicked back and shiny. He glanced back at his wife, sitting two rows behind him. She cried openly as he turned back to face the judge.

"Christopher Thibodaux," the judge intoned, "I hereby sentence you to life in a federal prison, with no possibility of parole, for the murder of Chief Ron Waldron."

Another round of whispers greeted the announcement, but fell silent under the judge's gavel.

"You are both hereby remanded to the Department of Corrections for placement in the Oakdale Federal Prison where you will serve your sentences."

Clapping could be heard scattered across the back of the courtroom. The judge frowned and tapped his gavel once more.

"Court is dismissed."

Thibodaux's wife tried to run after him as the guards escorted him to the back, but a wall of officers restrained her. Security had been tight throughout the proceedings, and Geoff breathed a sighed, relieved that it was over. He whispered a silent prayer for the Chief, happy that justice had been served.

Geoff walked out of the courtroom, ready to face the day. He would make the Chief proud, and serve the police force to the best of his ability, grateful for the town's support of its first black chief. The racism would stop here. As far as Geoff was concerned, the Klan was dead in his city.

* * *

Mathew Stephens collected items and packed them into a box. He stood back and looked at his former office in the courthouse, knowing it would never be his again. Although he had not been arrested or charged as a member of the KKK, rumors had forced him to resign. A new judge had already taken his seat. He went to the wall across from his desk and removed a framed degree, shoving it into the slim space still remaining in the box before carrying it to the wood-paneled door.

He took one last look around the room and carried the box down the wide hallway to the front of the courthouse, most people turned away from him, choosing not to notice that he was leaving. He didn't blame them; he had brought this disgrace upon himself, but now he needed to get on with his life. He started down the broad marble steps and in that moment, his heart froze.

Hannah was parked in front of the courthouse, leaning against the side of her car. After that brief moment of surprise, Mathew remembered to breathe again and continued down the steps to the long sidewalk. His heart beat heavily in his chest. Why was she here? Had she come to confront him... to gloat? Or maybe...

From this distance, he couldn't tell anything by the look on her face. He kept walking, but the sidewalk seemed to elongate, as though it were trying to keep him from her. As he drew near, he realized that she had been crying, and his heart ached for her. Then she smiled a tremulous smile and lifted her hand to wave. That was all the encouragement he needed as he practically ran the remaining few yards but stopped abruptly as he reached her, unsure of what to do.

"I didn't expect to see you here."

"I didn't expect to be here," she replied.

Mathew lifted a hand to catch a tear as it slowly slid down her soft brown skin. "You're crying. Why?"

"For all that has happened," she whispered. "I'm happy to see you."

She reached for him. He dropped the box and wrapped his arms tightly around her as she lifted her lips to his.

"I love you, Mathew Stephens," she murmured against his lips. "After what happened, I tried to deny it... but I couldn't."

He drank in her honeyed sweetness, inhaling the musky fragrance of her perfume and felt the familiar stirring of his body. He couldn't believe she was really here and that he wasn't dreaming.

"I love you, too, Hannah."

"So do you need a ride, stranger?" She dangled her keys in front of him and walked around the front of the car to open the

Gray Love

driver's side door. He retrieved his box of stuff, setting it on the back seat and got in next to her.

Hannah turned to him once they were seated in the car, a serious look on her face. "I need to know something, Mathew. Why did you lie to me?"

Mathew couldn't meet her gaze. He looked down at his hands, as if to blame them for his treachery.

"Mathew?" Her voice came softer, hesitant.

He knew he owed her an explanation. "I don't know."

"That's not fair." Her tears started again. "After all this time, I deserve an answer, or an explanation, or something."

"I was so afraid I would lose you," he murmured, "and that's the real truth of it."

"You could have," she said. "You almost did."

"I know we have some serious talking to do, but not here." Mathew grabbed her hand and kissed it. "I'm just happy you're here."

"Me, too," she said with a smile, pulling her hand back. "But I'll need my hand to drive."

They were quiet during the ride to his house. Mathew watched her profile, seeing new lines of worry and sorrow. She looked wiser, less trusting, and the change squeezed his heart. He knew he had caused at least some of those changes, and he swore to himself that he would make it up to her if it was the last thing he ever did.

Hannah gasped when they pulled up in front of his home. He was just as astonished; he had avoided staying at the house, preferring a small apartment in town. The beautiful home looked like a hurricane had swept through it, breaking windows and spreading debris across the porch and yard. The words 'nigger lover' had been sprayed across his front door in red paint.

Mathew sighed and climbed out of the car. *That's what you deserve*, he told himself grimly. *You helped foster this notion for many years.*

Hannah followed him to the front door. "You aren't going to stay here tonight, are you?" The concern on her face tugged a smile from his lips.

"Don't worry, babe." He drew his keys from his pocket and slid one into the front lock. "I won't stay, but I have important papers to get. It won't take long." He didn't have the heart to tell her he hadn't been able to stay here since their breakup, unable to live with his memories of shared meals, long talks, and passionate love making.

The house stirred, musty air pushing past them, escaping to the freedom of the open doorway. Mathew closed the door behind them and locked it before climbing the stairs to his room. He opened his closet door and knelt down, throwing everything on the floor aside. Removing a couple pieces of the hardwood flooring, he pulled out a small safe about the size of a shoebox.

He pointed to a chest at the end of the bed. "Hannah, please hand me that bag over there."

She brought it to him, watching him with large dark eyes. He settled the safe on the floor and concentrated on the combination. It had been a while, and he didn't get it on the first try. With a curse, he tried again.

"I'll have to get a room for tonight, at least," he said, not looking at her. "I've been staying at an apartment for the past two months, but the Klan found it so I can't go back there."

"I want to stay with you." Her words held defiance, anger and fear.

He shook his head. "It's too dangerous."

He unlocked the safe and pulled out a pistol, some papers, and last but not least, a thick stash of neatly wrapped cash.

Placing everything into the bag, he removed a couple of Polo shirts and two pairs of Dockers from the closet and tossed them inside, followed by clean socks and underwear, and his shaving gear. "Let's go."

He led the way downstairs, walking quickly. The tapping of Hannah's heels told him she was following. He stopped at the door and took one last look around. "Damn, I will miss this place," he sighed.

"Where's your car?"

"The Klan fire bombed it a couple weeks back. I've been using taxis to get around."

They hurried back to Hannah's car and got in.

Without speaking, she started the car and stepped on the gas, leaving a couple skid marks on the concrete drive as she backed onto the street. Before long, they were on the main highway, headed east out of town.

"Mathew, I'm frightened for both you and my family." Her eyes never left the road, but Mathew could hear the fear in her voice. "If I leave with you, if I leave them behind…" Her voice trailed off, and her eyes brimmed with unshed tears.

"I can't stay here, Hannah. I have no future left in this town." He said it gently, trying to ease the blow. She couldn't come with him; he wouldn't ask. "Your family needs you here. I understand that."

"The Klan won't stop," she said with a sob. "They'll try and find you. They've already been to our house, and I know they won't leave us alone."

He laid his hand over hers on the steering wheel for a brief moment. "I'll figure something out… we'll work this out, together."

She nodded, but a large tear slipped from the corner of her eye and ran down her creamy skin. Mathew wanted to hold her, and tell her that everything would be okay. But he wasn't sure he could say it without lying.

Twenty miles from town, they found a cheap trucker's motel, boasting twenty-five dollar rooms. Hannah went inside the office to pay for a room, while Mathew waited, hunched down in the car. He had grabbed a baseball cap at the house, and now he put it on, pulling it down over his eyes.

He watched Hannah go to the desk and ring the bell. After what seemed like an eternity, a tall, thin white man with a grizzled face came to the desk. She filled out a form and handed over some cash. The manager gave her a key and a leer, and she hurried back to the car.

When she entered the car, she looked upset, but simply dropped the keychain marked number eight in Mathew's lap and drove around the side of the building. Hannah parked in front of their unit, and Mathew hurried inside, clutching his bag. He closed and locked the door behind her and sighed with relief.

"It's still early," Hannah said. "It's barely one o'clock."

Mathew hugged her. "Thank you."

She turned away from his embrace, moving to stand in front of the window before drawing the drapes.

"What's wrong?" He stood behind her but wouldn't touch her again. Not until she was ready.

She turned and faced him, her dark eyes wide and fearful. "I'm afraid, Mathew."

Mathew took her hand and pulled her over to the bed. "Here, sit down." He waited until she settled herself, before sitting beside her, but not too close. "Listen, Hannah, I've been thinking." He squeezed her hand, wishing he could read her expression. "I want things to work out for us, but I can't stay here. I'm not a judge any longer."

"What are you going to do?" Her lips trembled. "Where are you going to go?"

"I'm thinking about going to New York. I have investments and plenty of money there, especially since I closed out all my accounts here in Mississippi. I won't have to worry, and once my property is sold, I'll have more. I can start teaching. I've always wanted to do that."

He had pricked her interest, and she focused more on what he was saying than the fear he had seen moments earlier.

"What held you back?"

Trust her to ask the hard questions. He took a deep breath. "To tell you the truth, it was the Klan. I don't know why I stayed with them for so long. Now that I look back on it, I can't believe how stupid I was."

Regret nearly overwhelmed him. He had not only ruined his life, but hers and many others as well. Did he deserve a new beginning? Did he deserve anything after all the things he had done? Somehow, it didn't feel right.

Hannah seemed to pick up on his thoughts, and she reached out for him. "Oh, baby." She sighed as she gave him a hug. Straightening, she gave him a brave smile. "How soon are you leaving for New York?"

"I don't know." He wasn't certain he could leave her. "Maybe next week." She said nothing, so he went on. "You could come with me. You wouldn't have any trouble finding a good job. You could even start your own law firm."

"I know that," she whispered. "But I have something more important to tell you, and I don't know how to say it."

Mathew reached for her hand again. "Just say it. Whatever the problem is, we can fix it together."

"That's the trouble, Mathew," she cried, her tears flowing again. "I don't want to fix it. We're going to have a baby."

All the breath left his body. "A baby?" Joy swept through him. "Really... Hannah... a baby?" Mathew could barely speak. "Why didn't you tell me sooner?" He stopped, rising abruptly. "You *were* going to tell me, *weren't* you?"

"No. I wasn't." She looked at him with hurt in her eyes.

"Why?"

Hannah wiped her tears with the back of her hand. "I was so scared," she said, counting on her fingers. "First, I didn't know if you were ready for something like this. And second, look at what happened when the wrong people found out about us. What do you think they would do if they knew I was carrying your child?"

"What happened? Did someone try to hurt you?"

"Two Klansmen in white robes came to my daddy's house. They were trying to scare us." He could hear the anger in her voice and watched her hands clench into fists.

"Hannah, I had no idea." He reached for her hands and pried them open, smoothing the warm skin with circular motions of his long, gentle fingers. How could he have subjected her and her family to such terrible things?

She laughed. It sounded bitter and harsh in the tiny room. "Why are you surprised? After all, you know them better than I do – their beliefs, and the things they're capable of. The whole point is this; it's 2009, yet certain people still care about the person you date... and the color of your skin, even though it is none of their business."

Mathew shook his head. "Not everyone."

"I hate to burst your bubble, but I am not some naïve child, you know." She glared at him, pulling her hands away from his touch. "Some whites hate blacks and some blacks hate whites, and let's not forget the other minority groups we degrade as well. Maybe all of us are a big group of racist, selfish bastards.

Gray Love

It's as bad in the South as it is in Iraq, only they try to keep everything hidden."

"Please, calm down." Mathew put all the sincerity he could muster into his voice. "I'm here for you. I want you to come to New York with me. I want to marry you and have a family. People in the north are a lot more accepting. I recently spent a couple weeks in New York, looking for an apartment and saw mixed couples every day and guess what? No one paid any attention to them."

He slid to the floor to land on one knee. Looking up at her, he reached for her hand, and she gave it to him. She couldn't help herself.

"Hannah, I know this isn't the best time, and God knows," he looked around the drab room, "this isn't the place, but I love you. Will you marry me?"

Hannah leaned forward to kiss him, wrapping her arms around his neck. Leaning close, she whispered into his ear, "I love you, too. And, yes, I will marry you."

Chapter Twenty-Seven

Hours passed before Hannah woke up. They had made love for hours, occasionally drifting off to sleep while holding each other as if afraid to let go. But after a brief nap, Mathew left the bed while she slept. When she later awoke, Hannah looked at her watch with a frown. Nearly five o'clock. Something smelled good, and she sought out the source. Pizza and a two-liter bottle of caffeine-free Coke sat on top of the battered chest of drawers. He must have stepped out while she was sleeping.

She pushed the covers aside and swung her feet to the floor, padding to the bathroom. Mathew stood in front of the mirror, a towel wrapped around his waist, his tanned skin glistening with moisture. He had wiped a clear spot on the foggy mirror to help him shave.

Hannah quietly watched as he groomed himself. He looked good, healthy and happier than he had a few short hours ago.

Mathew jumped when she touched his arm. He smiled down at her. "Good evening, sunshine." He gave her a quick peck on the lips. "I made dinner." He gestured to the pizza and Coke. "How about a picnic?"

Pouring the Coke into cheap plastic cups he had taken from the top of the dresser, he carried the box of pizza and two sodas to the bed, settling the drinks on the nightstand and the pizza in front of her before settling next to her.

"I think we need to lay low tonight," Mathew said.

"I agree. Let me call my parents and let them know I won't be home." She reached for the motel phone and dialed. "Ma, it's me."

Across the phone lines, she could hear her mother's relief. "Hannah, what's going on? Where are you? I was so worried when you didn't come home."

She quickly reassured her mother. "Don't worry, Ma. I just wanted to let you know I'm okay."

There was a moment of silence, and her mother asked, "Are you with Mathew?"

"Yes, Ma, but it isn't what you think."

"Hannah, I think you should come home." Her mother's words and tone were stern and firm. "When I was at the store earlier, I heard a couple townsfolk say the Klan is looking for him. I don't want you anywhere near him."

Hannah glanced over to where Mathew munched on a slice of pepperoni pizza and turned away, lowering her voice. "I'm a grown woman, Ma. I know how to take care of myself."

Her mother remained silent for a long time before saying, "You're right, Hannah. I trust your judgment. Just be careful. Promise me?"

"I promise." She hung up and dug into the pizza.

Around seven-thirty, Hannah heard voices outside. She leaned over to turn off the lights and the television. Mathew went to the window and peeked around the side of the drapes.

"There are men out there, at least five of them," he whispered over his shoulder. "I recognize Robert Hemming, a clerk from my court, and Bobby Robichaux, a local barber."

Hannah reached for her bra and panties, quickly slipping into each piece before donning her dress. "What's going on?"

Mathew shushed her. "It's a group of Klansmen. I'm trying to listen."

She stood beside him, slipping under his arm. He squeezed her gently, but his attention remained focused on the men near the office of the motel. "They're talking about me."

The voices became clearer. "We need to show him how we treat betrayers of the Klan." The man who said it brandished a wicked-looking, sawed-off shotgun. "Maybe we should pay his girlfriend a visit first."

Several of the men nodded, until another man spoke up. "Let's finish trashing the bastard's house and burn it to the ground. He's got some expensive stuff in there that will fetch a good price."

The men hooted and raised their guns high. The motel clerk, who earlier had checked Hannah in, was part of the group that jumped into an SUV and raced off.

"We have to go," Hannah said, grabbing her purse. "They're after my parents."

"Call them." Mathew hurried over to the phone.

"We don't have time." She dug her car keys out and reached for the door. Hannah ran out of the room, Mathew close behind, carrying his bag of valuables, which he threw in the trunk of the car.

"Let me drive."

She tossed him the keys and they peeled out of the motel parking lot, heading toward Hannah's house.

"Why don't you call your folks on your cell?" Mathew asked.

"It's on the charger at home. I walked off and forgot it this morning. If they finish up your house first, we may have time." She looked over at him, noting the fierce expression on his face. "But if they went directly there…"

"I know." He drove as fast as he dared.

Hannah couldn't say it, couldn't even think about what might happen if they didn't reach her parents in time. She didn't want them to be caught off guard. But when they turned the corner and onto her street, the Klan members were clearly visible in her parent's front yard, their white robes and eerie headgear sharply outlined by a burning cross and several torches.

"Damn, they got here in less than ten minutes." Mathew looked over at her. "I'm going to have to face them."

His declaration made Hannah realize that he loved her without a doubt, since he was willing to risk his life for her parents, even though he knew they didn't like him. His willingness to sacrifice himself made her love him all the more.

She thought quickly. "Pull in the alley over there and drive around back."

The car barreled down a short alley, running behind the houses on her family's side of the street, and stopped directly behind the Collins' house. Her mother's face peered out at them from the kitchen window.

Hannah jumped out and opened the back door, motioning to her mother. Within seconds, her parents ran out the back door, her father clutching a large bag to his broad chest. Her mother carried a small suitcase and her jewelry box.

Mrs. Collins slid into the back seat and reached for the bag her husband carried. He threw it in and slid in beside her. Hannah climbed in next to Mathew.

"They're back here," Bobby Robichaux yelled, coming around the side of the house. "Come on."

His voice carried in the evening stillness, and Hannah screamed at Mathew. "Go, go, go!"

Mathew slammed his foot against the accelerator, and the car sped down the alley and onto the street. As they careened around the corner, Hannah glanced at her father, who had turned for a final look at his home. Charlie knew that his house and business would be burned to the ground and held his wife close in his arms, his face angry and sad.

"Hannah," her mother cried, "they're burning down the house." Tears rolled down her face as she watched her home, filled with all of her finest memories, go up in flames.

Her father spoke up, his tone harsh. "Look at the evil your people have done, Mathew Stephens! You dirty bastard."

"Dad," Hannah shushed him, "they destroyed his home as well. Besides, he helped save you and Ma."

Mathew placed his hand on her leg, giving her a sad smile. "No, Hannah, I deserved that."

He glanced at her father in the rearview mirror, and took a deep breath. "I am truly sorry, sir. I will buy you another home wherever you want."

"I sure as hell don't need your money," her father growled. "We have plenty of our own, and the insurance company will cover the losses."

Deborah Collins reached for his hand. "Give the boy a chance, Charlie."

Hannah met her mother's eyes, and they exchanged a gentle smile.

Mrs. Collins went on. "Give him a chance to speak and make amends."

"Please, Daddy." Hannah leaned over the front seat and reached for her father's hand. After a moment, he took her hand and squeezed it, his frown lessening just a bit.

"Then let him tell me what he's done." He sat back and shifted the bag from his lap to the floor. "I've got every paper, stock, bond, and checkbook I own in this bag. It looks like we're on the run now, too, all because of him."

Mathew kept his eyes focused on the road, but Hannah saw his jaw tighten. His features steadied as a look of determination took hold, but his voice held steady. "Sir, I love your daughter more than life itself, and there's nothing I want more than to make her happy, except maybe to get your approval for our marriage."

Her father snorted, but Mathew kept talking. "I hope you will give us your blessing, but even if you don't, I am going to marry her."

There was a long, uncomfortable silence in the car, and Hannah was afraid to break it. She silently prayed, hoping Mathew's sincerity was as apparent to her father as it was to her. Still, she kept her eyes forward, and waited for him to say something, anything to show how he felt about Mathew's statement.

"Well, I guess you had better decide where we're going, then." Her father's words fell between them, and Hannah smiled. She wanted to laugh, and run, and scream her joy to the world. Finally, everything was going to be all right.

Chapter Twenty-Eight

Mathew drove more than ninety miles out of the state. When he stopped to get gas, Hannah was asleep, and so were her parents.

He put his credit card in the slot and stuffed the nozzle into the gas tank. Hannah woke up and climbed out of the car moments later, leaning against the passenger door to watch him.

"Do you have any clue as to where we're going?"

He smiled, taking in the warm flush of her face and her beautiful hair falling around her cheeks. "I figure we would drive for another three hours until we're out of Mississippi. Then we can grab a hotel and decide what to do next."

Hannah's parents stirred in the back of the car, and her mother spoke up. "Well, Charlie, I never thought it would come to this, but I guess it's something we have to do now."

"If we're leaving the state, I say we head for Chicago," her father said, leaning out the window. "I've always wanted to visit that city."

Mathew finished pumping gas and screwed the lid on before climbing back into the car. Hannah got in again. He looked at her and then over the seat to where her parents sat.

"Chicago, huh? Once we get to a hotel, we have to decide what to do."

Her father grunted. "Deborah and I have been talking about visiting Chicago for some time now. I just didn't think it would happen like this."

Mrs. Collins nodded, but her face still held sadness. "Where were you planning to go, Mathew? Will the two of you join us there, or did you have something else in mind?"

"I decided to head for New York." Mathew watched their faces as he said it.

Hannah's father looked relieved. "At least you're going somewhere away from here."

Mathew glanced at Hannah, and she turned around. "I'm going with him."

"Lord Jesus," her father said with a sigh.

"Hannah, are you sure about this?" her mother asked.

Hannah looked at Mathew, her face alight with love and nodded. "Very sure."

Her mother sighed, and reached for her husband's hand. Charlie gave Mathew a hard look.

"And you're going to be grandparents," Hannah said, a huge grin on her face.

A frown started across her father's brow, and he leaned forward. "You had better take good care of my baby, or there will be hell to pay," he told Mathew.

Mathew knew then that it would be all right. He would have a family, a new life, the woman he loved, and her parents would be wonderful grandparents.

He saluted. "Yes, sir."

Reaching for the key, he started the car and pulled back onto the road.

Four hours later, they arrived in Birmingham, Alabama. They found a Sheridan Hotel to rest for the day until they figured out what to do. Mathew checked them into a room, and they sat in silence, two on each double bed, as if no one knew quite what to say.

"Hannah, are you okay?" her father asked, his face concerned.

She nodded and reached for Mathew's hand. "Yes, I think so."

Deborah went to Hannah and embraced her. "I was so worried about you."

Hannah returned her mother's hug, and pulled her down next to her on the bed. "It'll be okay. Mathew will take good care of me."

Her father spoke up from where he sat propped against the pillows of the other bed. "What is Hannah going to do about work? She's a great attorney."

"I'm sure I won't have any trouble finding work with a good firm in New York. Besides, I'll have a better opportunity for advancement in whatever firm hires me." She smiled at her father, knowing he found it difficult to let go and to admit she didn't need him to protect her any longer.

Mathew turned to her father. "Mr. Collins, I love your daughter and intend to marry her. I have plenty of money set aside, so you don't have to worry. She'll have the best of everything."

"I don't want my little girl going to New York," her father said suddenly. "Her mother and I need her with us."

Mrs. Collins got up and moved to the other bed to sit beside her husband, reaching for his hand. "Well, honey," she said, "we have some money, too. I know you like the idea of visiting Chicago, but we could go to New York with them."

Hannah felt like she would burst with excitement. Missing her parents was the only thing she had worried about, and now they might be going with her. "Oh, Ma, that would be wonderful. This way, you can see your new grandchild as often as you wish."

"Then we head for New York?" Mathew asked expectantly.

She smiled. "New York it is."

"It's not like we have anything to lose, Deborah," her father conceded. "I always wanted to go to New York, too."

"I'm glad that's settled," Deborah Collins said, getting up from the bed and pulling her husband up with her. "Your father and I will be downtown. We've got a bit of shopping to do."

When her parents left the room, Mathew folded Hannah into his arms. "How are you feeling?" he asked, pressing his lips against her hair.

Hannah pulled back enough to kiss him. "Fine, too bad we're sharing a room," she said teasingly.

"Don't tempt me, woman," he said with a mock growl, pinching her bottom. "Besides, I've got some calls to make. We need airline tickets and a place to stay, before we're ready to begin our new life together."

Hannah nodded. Her heart was full to bursting as Mathew reached for the phone, and she knew that their future would be bright and happy.